The
Judgment

The
Judgment
The Impact Series

C K Westbrook

4 Horsemen
Publications, Inc.

4 Horsemen
Publications, Inc.

4 Horsemen Publications, Inc.
1497 Main St. Suite 169
Dunedin, FL 34698
4horsemenpublications.com
info@4horsemenpublications.com

Cover by J. Kotick
Typesetting by Niki Tantillo
Edited by S.L. Vargas

Library of Congress Control Number: 2022949680

Paperback ISBN-13: 978-1-64450-712-4
Hardback ISBN-13" 978-1-64450-852-7
EBook ISBN-13: 978-1-64450-713-1
Audiobook ISBN-13: 978-1-64450-714-8

For Chelsea

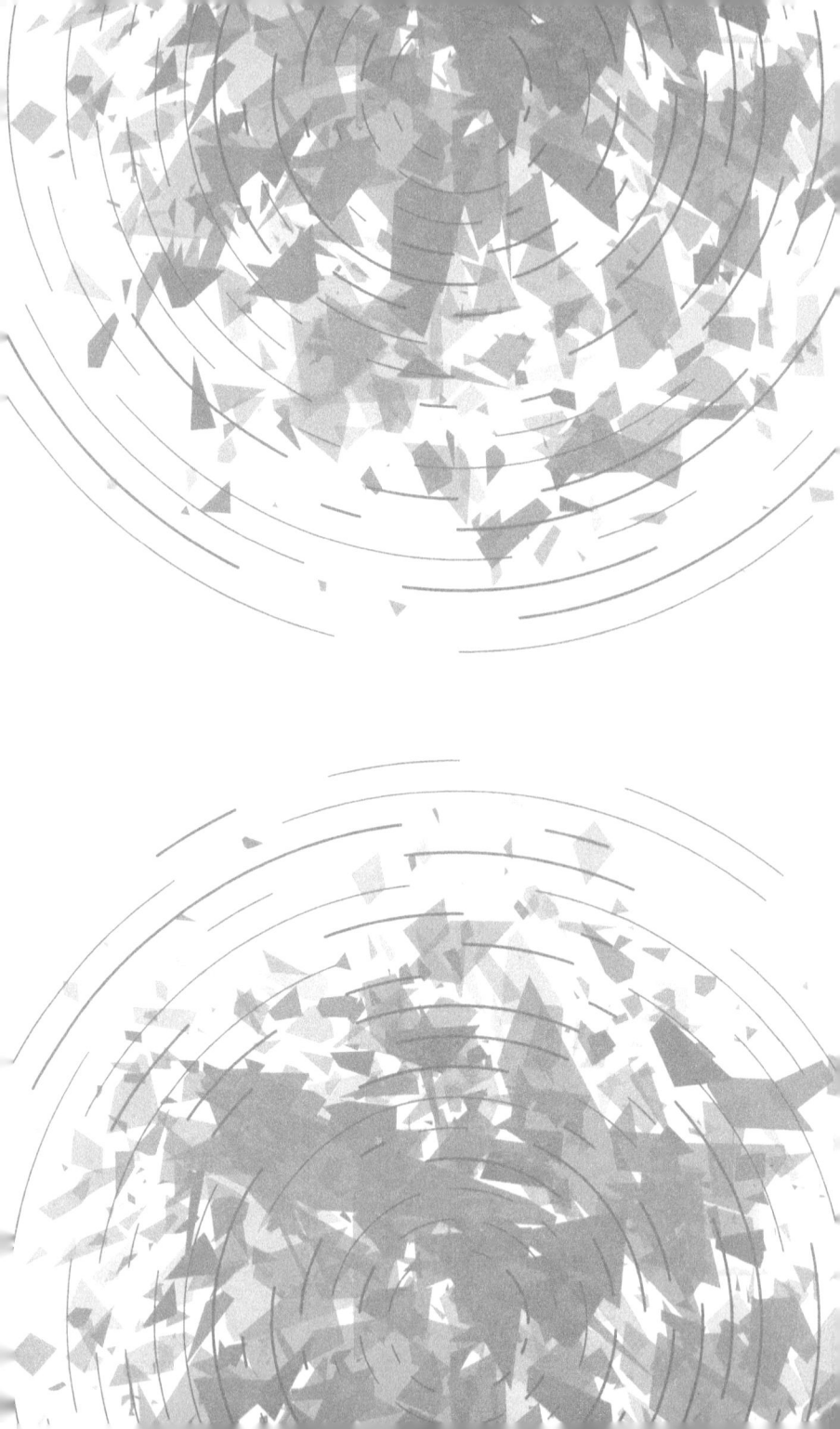

ACKNOWLEDGEMENTS

I must thank 4 Horsemen Publications for their continued support of me and this series. Val, Jen, Erika, and Beau have made me an author and taught me how to publish novels and I am extremely grateful. This time, I'm not only thanking Chelsea for her help in bringing these stories into the world, but I'm also dedicating this book to her. I can't think of a better way to honor her contributions to this series. I must thank Denise again for her support, friendship, and sharing of her expertise and experience in many fields. I am immensely grateful to my sisters, Shana and Jess, for their continued assistance, encouragement, and love through this process. I sincerely appreciate my silent writing partners, Skye and Bruichladdich, for always being close and entertaining. I'm forever grateful for Jeffrey, the best decision I ever made. He is always patient, supportive, and there to help me out of a block with a kind word or excellent suggestion, and he has read these stories too many times to count. And once again, my most profound gratitude is to my readers who have joined me on this amazing Impact Series adventure. Thank you!

Table of Contents

ONE

Fifty-Nine Days After the Shooting

"Oh my God. Rex, I'm so sorry," Kate said, putting her hands over her mouth in surprise. VIPs in his world had died in the collision that brought Rex and his wrath to Earth, but everything had become more complicated with the new knowledge that his parents were those very VIPs.

"I love my mom so much; I can't imagine the pain if I lost her. I am so, so sorry." Kate brushed away the fat tears that started to pour out of her eyes. "I wish I could give you a hug."

"It's okay, Kate. We don't experience comfort from touch the way you do," Rex slowly replied.

Kate was in the white room, where the walls, floor, and ceiling were all white, making it hard to tell how large the room was. Kate stared at the human-sized orange cat across the room and nodded. *Oh right. That's just some kind of avatar anyway. I don't know where Rex is. Or what he is.*

She wiped her tears with her shirt. She patted her running shorts, wishing she had a tissue with her. She briefly considered using her crumpled pandemic running mask to blow her nose. The conversation was so shocking that Kate did not notice the temperature change. Or perhaps she had been in the white room so often that her body regulated itself faster. She was warm enough to remain standing comfortably, but the wave of empathetic pain was so heavy she sat back down on the floor, wrapping her arms around her knees.

"Would you please tell me what happened? What exactly caused the collision? You keep saying the dangerous pollution, and I understand that humans have left extremely dangerous debris all over space, but what exactly happened to your parents?" Kate asked.

Just a few moments ago, Kate was running down the beach looking for dolphins and feeling almost euphoric because they had thwarted new, additional global violence. The sky was full of clouds and explosions of beautiful color as the sun rose above the Atlantic Ocean. Crabs scampered about and birds flew out of her path when she got too close. Everything seemed calm and normal.

It was hard to imagine what Rex and the others would do next after making hundreds of millions of gun owners shoot themselves as punishment for polluting space. But working together, she, Sinclair, Jo-Ellen, and Rex had cleaned up space, making it safe for humans and others. Now she sat, hugging herself to keep from shaking. And not shaking from the cold, but heartbreaking sadness and fear of what Rex would say next.

How long will our alliance last?

A few minutes passed and then an image appeared. Kate stood to get a closer look. It showed Earth and millions of white lights, which surrounded the planet and expanded out into space.

"Are those lights? Or are they stars?" Kate asked confused. "It can't be debris! With your help, it's been pulverized. We got rid of the garbage! Space should be black and clean again. Right?" Her voice rose in disbelief and frustration.

"Yes, Kate. The debris was removed. This is what Earth looked like when my parents passed by. So much debris. No other planet has surrounded itself with pollution. They knew to be careful, of course. We are all familiar with cometary and asteroidal material and other natural substances. My parents must have been distracted by a tool bag that nearly hit a dead satellite. It's all recorded in the energy file. Their last words. Their last thoughts. They were just very confused by the enormous amount of garbage. They were discussing it—trying to figure out *why*. They thought maybe Earth had some trouble. Maybe it was in distress. The debris was not moving like the meteorite particles that exist throughout the universe," Rex said in his slow manner.

Kate thought of her mother, her sense of adventure, curiosity, and thoughtfulness. How incredibly painful it would be to relive the final moments of one's parents' lives, especially when it ended in such a shocking way.

No wonder Rex has a vested interest in cleaning up the debris. He doesn't want others to suffer the same loss he has.

After a long pause, Rex continued. "Cautiously, my parents moved closer. Then the two tiny pieces hit each other, causing a chain reaction involving some of the other 128 million pieces of debris. Enormous damage was caused by something smaller than one centimeter in diameter. One piece hit their transport at 18,000 miles per hour. The impact destabilized their craft and caused an explosion. They were ejected into space with damaged gear, causing them to expire. It happened very fast." Rex spoke slowly and calmly. "I determined that one of the tiny pieces was human waste—frozen urine—that hit a tiny shard of glass from a previous collision."

Another tear ran down Kate's cheek. "I'm so, so sorry, Rex. I know it sounds trite, but I don't know what else to say," she said. "I wish it hadn't happened. I wish they were alive. I wish humans weren't so careless."

"As do I," Rex said after a couple of silent minutes had passed.

A sudden memory flashed across Kate's mind. She and Sinclair were driving from Virginia to Texas before they changed course after learning that the collision debris was in Florida. She recalled the terror and disbelief she felt watching a Tesla fall from the sky and bounce into an adjacent field, very close to the highway they were driving on.

"Okay. Now I understand the toolkit on Jack's car. But why did the Tesla fall out of the sky near me and

Sinclair? Of all the garbage up there, why the Tesla?" Kate asked.

"You and Sinclair were in a car. And you like Teslas," Rex replied.

Kate did not really understand but moved on. There were more important things to discuss and understand. "And the others are coming to check on you? To make sure you're okay?"

"I came to Earth fast. I saw and understood what happened to my parents. I saw it in their energy. I witnessed the collision. I witnessed the ejection. But like them, I could not understand why there was so much debris—so much dangerous garbage floating around your planet. It was confusing to watch humans send ships and astronauts into a minefield they created. I wondered if your astronauts were being punished. Was there a war? Was there a catastrophic crisis? It took me a long time to understand," Rex droned.

"What did you understand?" Kate asked as a feeling of dread washed over her.

"Earth was not being attacked. There was no significant war in your world that would explain a desperate and potentially deadly exit from the planet," Rex explained.

"No. There is not," Kate said sadly, though, at times, the pandemic felt like a world war. And she and Kyle had been terrified that the narcissistic President would push the country into one.

"I watched and I learned. Humans are extremely selfish and many are vastly stupid. They lack imagination and creativity. Every single action has a reaction. Every choice has a consequence. They are presented with this information many times each day but they reject it. It is the strangest behavior I have seen throughout my travels," Rex said.

Kate encountered frustration over this all the time. "Yep. It's called cognitive dissonance or just self-delusion. And I would not say they lack imagination; they just use it wrong. Humans are quite capable of blaming *other* people for their garbage, pollution, and other problems. They blame corporations or the government or another race, sex, nationality, state, political party, or their parents. They create bad guys and elaborate conspiracies in their minds. They do mental calisthenics to ensure they don't have to take any personal responsibility. And it's ubiquitous —in every country, every town," Kate said quietly, feeling more depressed and defeated. She sat down on the floor, tired from the weight of all the sadness.

Humans are terrible parasites in so many ways. I wonder if he realizes we have polluted Earth far more than space. We have spread our deadly garbage everywhere, in cities, forests, lagoons, rivers, the deepest parts of the oceans, the tallest mountains, jungles, deserts, and prairies. Everywhere.

Kate laid on her back, resting her head on her hands, and stared up at the image of Earth surrounded by millions of pretty little lights which was really deadly garbage. She wanted to show Rex that she would stay as long as he would let her. She did not want him to send her back until she understood everything. She had been running on the beach when he snatched her up, so neither her mom nor Sinclair would miss her anytime soon.

Rex replayed the collision over and over. As Kate watched, she realized the playback had no sound because the collision would not have made a sound.

"Space seems so quiet," Kate said, watching the slow-motion collision on repeat. "I feel like it should sound something like that kilonova in 2017. That really started it, I think. I still don't like to think about it because I work in the space industry. Even though I work for the government and not corporate space, I'm very aware that I'm part of the problem."

"Started what?" Rex asked.

"The modern space race. The new billionaire boy corporate space race. When those neutron stars collided and merged or created a black hole, no one knows for sure exactly what they became, but we do know what they released: gold, platinum, and other minerals. I think that is what space exploration is really all about now. That, and getting rich people to a safe planet when they are done trashing this one," Kate said through clenched teeth, anger displacing her sadness.

"Yes. I studied Earth and realized there was no particular war or a specific and immediate threat to its existence. Just the desire to consume and discard. Everywhere, from almost all humans all over the planet. And they take pleasure in violence and death. A confusing species. A perplexing planet," Rex said.

Kate nodded sadly. *Okay, he does understand the scope of the problem.* "Don't blame the planet. Earth is just as much a victim here as you are. The Earth has provided everything for us: food, water, shelter, sun, tulips, dolphins, buffalo—"

"—oceans, waterfalls, moss, icebergs, dragonflies, lions, volcanoes, moose, and roses," Rex finished. "It's a beautiful planet. I have never seen anything like it. The colorful energy explodes everywhere."

"And humans trash it. It's never enough. They must consume more and more *and more*. Greed is a disease. The poor think only the rich are greedy and the rich think the same of the poor. The middle class think of themselves as harmless victims of the system. The American obsession with consumption has spread globally," Kate said.

This is not helping. I'm just making myself angry.

Kate suddenly sat up and looked at Rex. He flicked his tail. "Tell me about your parents. Why were they here?" Kate asked.

"That does not matter now," Rex murmured.

"What do you mean? Just because they died? Of course they matter! I would love to hear about them. What was their work? Why were they such beloved leaders? Were they fun parents? I want to hear everything," Kate said.

Kate wished Sinclair was with her. Sinclair had looked for life beyond Earth his whole life. The collision, the mass shooting, and the killing of hundreds of millions of people were such tragic ways to learn his research was right. *I really wish he were here with me to learn why it all happened.* "Please tell me about them. What were they doing so close to Earth?"

Rex was quiet for a long time, longer than his usual long pauses.

It occurred to Kate that she was being insensitive. "I'm sorry, Rex. If you don't want to talk about them,

I understand. But sometimes talking about loss does help. It helped me when my dad died."

"I took several months to understand. I decided to create what you refer to as the mass shooting because it did not hurt nature nor Earth. I decided that humans destroying themselves with their own weapons was the fairest punishment," Rex said slowly.

A chill ran down Kate's spine and she shivered.

"Yes. I mean, 70,000,000 dead Americans and hundreds of millions worldwide was very brutal, but I guess I kind of understand. Karma. Live by the gun, die by the gun," Kate said hesitantly. Yvette's—Sinclair's deceased wife's—face flashed in her mind. "Of course, there are many suffering from losing loved ones, so you kind of punished everyone," Kate added, remembering Sinclair's and Karisma's devastated faces.

"Humans killed my kind with their carelessness, their selfishness—I responded in kind," Rex said, faster than normal.

Fear pitted her stomach. *Is he getting angry?*

"They won't spend time learning or understanding. They may not accept my work. They might want more violence. They will be here soon," Rex continued in the fastest cadence Kate had ever heard him use.

"Wait. What? Who? How soon?" Kate had been so caught up with the conversation she forgot why Rex pulled her up in the first place: to tell her if their plan had worked. If the leaders of his world were still coming, they were still pissed off. The plan had failed.

"Soon," Rex repeated. "They are moving fast."

"Let me guess: in five days?" Kate snarled.

Rex said nothing for a minute.

"What's the worst-case scenario? What are they capable of doing? That is, if they don't accept the enormous death and pain and suffering you have caused and the incredible clean-up job we have accomplished together," Kate said.

"Maybe they will accept it," Rex conceded.

Kate stood up and began to pace. The video image of the collision disappeared.

Finally, she sighed. "What if they don't? What are they capable of doing to us?"

Rex did not speak for a long time.

I really wish Sinclair were here! Sinclair had been pulled into this white room once before. Rex had pulled them both up when they were running away from the cops and Space Force at Kennedy Space Center. That was just over a week ago, but it felt much longer because so much had happened since then. She was used to Rex's slow way of speaking and had learned to be patient, but Sinclair was better at coming up with technical solutions. She'd come to rely heavily on her astrophysicist neighbor over the last six turbulent weeks.

"You need to gather Sinclair and your mom and whomever else you value. I can bring them up to safety before the violence resumes. Let me know who you want to bring with you. I will be ready," Rex said.

"What the hell? Like a *list*? Like you will bring us up here or we will die? How much time? When? Why?" Kate asked, her voice growing louder with each question. Did she have minutes, hours, days? How wide of a net could she cast?

The floor started to shake.

"No, Rex! Wait! Please! I need to know more!" Kate shouted, just before landing in a superhero posture on the soft, hot sand where he'd found her.

TWO

Fifty-Nine Days After the Shooting

Kate yelled skyward, stomping up and down the beach. "Please! Bring me back up! Keep talking to me!" Sweat dripped off her brow. Between the perspiration, the tears, and the hot Florida sun, her mask was soaked. What had Rex meant by gathering the people close to her? What the hell was going to happen? She needed more information. Frantic, she started to run at a pace she usually couldn't sustain, yelling Rex's name with each thump of her sneaker on the sand.

A few passersby looked her way; others ignored her completely. She looked and sounded insane, but she didn't care.

After an hour of running, looking up in the sky, calling his name, she gave up. Exhausted and thirsty, she slowly walked back to her mom's condo, anxious and defeated. She walked inside to find Sinclair making coffee. He looked at her quizzically, his brows furrowed over his big brown eyes.

"How was your run, Kate?" Sinclair asked, lifting one eyebrow.

"Okay," Kate replied, trying to channel a calmness she didn't feel, but she didn't want to worry her mom. Hands shaking, she poured a glass of water and plopped down in a chair at the kitchen table.

"How about some coffee?" Sinclair asked, putting a cup in front of her. "Or maybe you're jittery enough." She followed his gaze down to her violently trembling hands. "Have you been crying?"

"Where's my mom?" Kate asked, her voice sounding high-pitched and tense to her own ears.

"Jackie went to her friend's house. Lourdes, I think that was the name. She said she'd be gone a few hours." He sat down at the table, his gaze intense. "What happened? You seem upset. You're not the bubbly, We-Saved-The-World-Kate you were when you set out for your run. You were gone a long time. I know you've been crying. Did you see Rex?"

Kate just nodded.

"I gather we failed," Sinclair said, his lips pressed into a grim line. "They're coming anyway."

"I need to write down our conversation before I forget the details," Kate said, jumping up from the table and looking around for paper and a pen. After she found them, she sat down and started to write.

1. Rex told the others the debris was pulverized—but they are coming anyway.

2. Rex does not know if our ploy worked.

3. They are concerned Rex has been here too long.

4. The important VIPs that died were his parents.

5. He showed me what they saw: the debris, the pee, the collision, the explosion, the ejection.

6. He doesn't know what they plan to do to us or Earth when they arrive

7. Rex said to get Sinclair, mom, and whomever else I value so Rex can bring them up before the violence starts.

8. They are coming fast, soon (maybe five days—my guess, not Rex's words).

"Yep, I think that sums it up," Kate announced, sliding the paper across the table to Sinclair.

"Holy shit," Sinclair murmured as he read the list. "What the hell? This is not good!"

He jumped out of his chair and paced the small kitchen, waving the slip of paper as he spoke. "Let me get this straight. We used the debris that we found at

Kennedy Space Center to make a fake advanced laser prototype that was meant to destroy all the dangerous space debris. We managed to get the tech launched into space. We created a perfect illusion so that Rex could destroy the debris while making it look like we humans did it. But they knew it was a ruse? They're still angry?"

Kate read the panic on his face. "I know, right? What the fuck? Swear words are totally appropriate right now. I mean, we did all that work; risked getting COVID, killed, or arrested; and it seems like it was all for nothing. I mean, if the end of the world is imminent anyway, it was all for nothing!" Kate was still shaking, but she had to pull herself together. "Listen, I'm sweaty and sandy and I need to take a shower."

I look horrible. I need to think this through. And I don't want to lose it in front of Sinclair.

As Kate stood, Sinclair approached her. "Not so fast." He took her in his arms and hugged her tight for a long time. As he released her, he took her hands and stared deeply into her eyes.

A bolt of lightning hit her chest.

"You're amazing, Kate. We figured out a solution before; maybe we can again. Don't give up." He pulled her back in for another hug. "This is a lot for one person to handle. I wish Rex had taken me up with you."

"Me too. You would have asked better questions. You wouldn't have cried so much," Kate mumbled into his chest, tears of frustration dampening his shirt.

She didn't want to pull away from Sinclair. She felt safe here, with him. Reassured by the steadiness of his breath and the feeling of his strong arms around her. Kate sighed. Still, she was frustrated with herself; she must look terrible with her eyes all red and swollen, and she really needed to blow her nose. She was also worried her mom would walk in and see her so upset. Reluctantly, she stepped back and ran to the bathroom before he could entice her with another hug.

Kate was not ready to tell her mom about the latest death threat. *Not until I have a plan.*

THREE

Fifty-Nine Days After the Shooting

After Kate finished showering and dressed, she felt calmer. No more tears. No more trembling. She needed a solid plan and to take action. But what to do next?

Make a list of the people I love most. Mom, of course. And Sinclair.

Her face got hot just thinking of putting Sinclair on that list, but of course, he had to be on it. He'd helped avert disaster the first time around. Well, at least temporarily. Plus, she was very fond of him.

In the living room, she found her mom and Sinclair sitting and talking.

Her mom's eyes were red and tears slid down her cheeks.

Our tendency to cry runs in the family.

"What's wrong?" Kate asked, quickly glancing out the front window to see if there was any unusual activity or violence.

Sinclair jumped up. "Jackie is upset about Lourdes. Everything else is fine. Well, I mean, all things considered. It's natural for Lourdes to be upset. She is mourning."

"Yes. I was telling Sinclair that Lourdes lost her husband and oldest son in the shooting. It was so tragic. Sometimes, I really hate Rex." Her mom sighed loudly. "Lourdes has been my best friend almost since the day I arrived in Florida. She was a new teacher at the school too. She was a single mom with a son around Kate's age. Michael—his name was Michael. She has a daughter, Hailey, a few years younger than Kate. We muddled through life together. Dealt with bad principals together. Helped each other be better teachers and parents. Lourdes remarried a few years ago." Kate's mom took a deep breath and reached for a tissue. "Her husband, Carlos, died in the shooting. She lost Carlos and Michael on the same day."

"I know, Mom. It's terrible. Mike was such a nice guy. My heart breaks for Lourdes." Kate sat down on the couch next to her mom. She put her arm around her mom's shoulders and pulled her close. "How are she and Hailey holding up?"

"They aren't doing well. The house is a mess. Lourdes was never big on housework, but there is sadness, a really deep depression to the mess now. It's bad. As we unloaded groceries together, I started to clean up the kitchen. It took a couple of hours to pull it together. Lots of empty wine and rum bottles. I plan to go back tomorrow after you guys leave. I need to really dig in and help get them organized," Jackie said.

"That's really nice, Mom. You're a great friend," Kate said. Her mother was a true saint who never shied away from cleaning up others' messes.

"Not really. I was so busy with the orphans—Jake, Leia, and baby Katniss—I didn't realize Lourdes and Hailey weren't doing okay. I didn't realize how much things were falling apart for them. Then I left town for a week to get the kids settled with relatives in Tennessee. I am a terrible friend. She needed me. She needs me." Her mom buried her face in a wad of tissues.

Kate traced hearts on her mom's back, shushing her. "Come on, Mom. You were helping the kids find a safe home. You were helping me and Sinclair unwind after a nerve-wracking and dangerous adventure. You're amazing and doing the best you can. Lourdes knows this. She loves you."

"Lourdes helped me when the kids first arrived. She didn't want to foster children because she didn't feel she could while dealing with her own loss. She did take in a few dogs and cats that lost their owners. Very sweet, but that has also contributed to the mess," Jackie admitted. With a deep breath, she rolled her shoulders back in a gesture Kate recognized as her getting her emotions together. "Anyway, I will head over in the morning and help. I feel better being busy and not sitting here alone, missing you."

Sinclair stood, arms crossed, like he was trying to give them space. Just minutes ago, he'd been the one comforting her and now she was comforting her mom. What a mess. What a mess they were all in. Would they soon have to leave? Could Kate get Lourdes and her family on Rex's list? Was there a cap on how many people she could bring? And what about Kyle? Her boyfriend had been nothing but supportive since this crisis began, and it had just now occurred to her to put him on the list.

"Why don't you go back over to Lourdes' this afternoon?" Kate suggested, trying to keep her tone light. "Sinclair and I will shop and cook dinner. We'll make a nice farewell dinner. You can invite Lourdes and Hailey here. Plus, Sinclair and I need a little time to organize the car and create a COVID-safe plan for our drive back to D.C. Though I bet we can pack in five minutes flat. We'll just shove our latest Target purchases into one shared bag."

Memories of her and Sinclair driving away from the hysterical mob in D.C., with only the clothes on their backs, flashed through her mind. She hadn't done much shopping, just surviving day by day. *Was that mob attack just eleven days ago?*

"That actually sounds good. Would that be okay? I really wanted us to spend your last day together," Jackie asked.

Kate noticed her mom's hair had gotten grayer, almost as if it happened overnight. The stress was taking a toll on all of them. Kate squeezed her mom's knee. "We'll have a nice dinner together. And you won't have to spend the afternoon worrying about Lourdes because you'll be with her." She got up from the couch

"Okay," Jackie said. "I will go and bring them back here around 7:00 pm. Just do something simple.

Maybe grill some vegetables and make a big salad. They seem like they need some healthy food."

"We are on it, mom. No problem." Kate walked her mom to the front door. "See you later."

As soon as the door closed, Kate leaned her back against it and shut her eyes. "I feel terrible for Lourdes and Hailey and the foster pets, but I am so glad mom is distracted. I worried she would figure out that I'm upset. Moms can tell. I don't want to dump this crisis on her yet."

Even with her eyes closed, she could sense Sinclair had moved closer to her. "Makes sense. Not a word to anyone until we know what we're facing and have a plan to execute. And Kate, you're not alone in this," Sinclair said, his voice sending a quick shiver up her spine.

When she opened her eyes, the intensity of his gaze shook her. "Uh, let's go get some groceries and plan an amazing meal. Hell, it could be our last," Kate replied with a nervous laugh, suddenly feeling awkward and self-conscious.

Stop it, Kate. Don't be ridiculous. Sinclair was just doing his part for humanity. His involvement had nothing to do with feelings for her. And even if it did, she had a fantastic and supportive boyfriend waiting at home.

They drove to an almost empty grocery store and went to a farmers' market that housed only one lonely stand that stocked some delicious local produce.

"Let's buy a cooler and fill it with fruits and vegetables and hummus for our long drive. More natural vitamins and good stuff and fewer gas station sandwiches," Kate suggested on the way back to Jackie's condo.

"Great idea," Sinclair said, turning the car around to go back to the stores.

"Sorry, I did not think of it earlier. I feel distracted and scattered. I keep seeing the image of the collision over and over. Rex's warning keeps going through my mind. I can't stop looking up at the sky, worried something will fall. And maybe this time it will land on us because it will not be sent by Rex," Kate said.

"No worries. I feel the same way, distracted and hyper." Sinclair's knuckles whitened on the wheel. "But I do feel better moving and doing stuff. I feel like my subconscious is working. Any minute now, I will have some deep insight into the situation."

He missed the entrance to the shopping center. "Or not," he added with a smile as he made yet another U-turn.

FOUR

Sixty Days After the Shooting

They'd been on the road for an hour and Kate was still brushing tears off her face thinking about the dinner the night before. *So much for trying not to look red and puffy in front of Sinclair all the time,* Kate thought as she reached for a tissue in the glove compartment. Her mother and Lourdes were so close they finished each other's stories. There was a lot of laughter. Even Hailey, despite her depression, seemed to enjoy herself.

Stop crying. We are still alive. The sky is blue, the sun is shining, and Sinclair is with me. We have a long drive home to think and plan. Well, assuming we actually have five days.

"That was so fun last night," Kate said, staring out at the near-empty road. "And the food was a hit. No one even mentioned it was all vegan. I mean, I know they all knew, but I think it was so delicious that the meat-eaters didn't even miss flesh. The wine and dessert were fantastic. How lucky we are to get great food and wine in a pandemic, in the aftershock of a worldwide mass shooting, in a state that took such a huge hit! We are very, very lucky." Maybe the more she counted what was good right now, she'd stop thinking about the bad that was coming.

"And how fortunate to spend time with your mother and her friends. Everyone seemed to have a well-deserved relaxing night. Lourdes joking about losing her mind and the crazy things she and Hailey have been doing was not just funny, but, I think, cathartic," Sinclair wisely noted.

Kate took a big breath. "I agree. They'll be okay. They'll make it through this terrible, tragic time." Another wave of emotion nearly doubled her over.

Sinclair reached for her hand and kissed her knuckles. "It's going to be okay, Kate. We are going to figure this out."

Heat rushed through her body. That was a platonic kiss, but it didn't matter. It was kind and sincere and made her feel warm all over.

Obviously, she was just missing her boyfriend.

"So why all the tears?" Sinclair asked.

"I just hated saying goodbye this morning. And I feel bad for not telling my mom everything, but she and everyone have been through so much. She doesn't need to deal with another crisis horror-story nightmare," Kate said, wiping away fresh tears.

Was that the last time I will ever hug my mom?

Sinclair's hand, still holding hers, rested on her thigh. "It's going to be okay, Kate. We'll figure this out. I support that you didn't tell Jackie. What good would it do to have more people worry about things they can't control? But, you know, you could use a break from this crisis horror-story nightmare as well." He picked her hand back up and held it to his chest.

"But we're not getting a break," Kate said, reaching for a tissue with her free hand and wiping away fresh tears.

Here I am again, all red and splotchy, with a snotty nose. No matter what, Sinclair always seems calm and handsome. How does he control his emotions?

"I feel like I have been crying since July 14. Like every single day, just constantly crying. I should be suffering from severe dehydration. But it's enough. No more tears. I need to focus," Kate said, taking several deep breaths. "We are in a major crisis and I need to pull it together. And I have an idea." She released Sinclair's hand and reached for her phone. She typed in silence for several minutes.

"Okay, I think I have it. Or, at least, a good first draft. I will read it to you, and we can edit and revise it together. We have a fourteen-hour drive to get it right," Kate said, looking at her phone.

"What is it?" Sinclair asked quizzically, momentarily taking his eyes off the road to look at the phone screen.

"My list for Rex. So far it includes you, Jackie, Kyle, Karisma, Harriet, Kyle's parents and siblings, three of my best friends and their significant others and their kids, Jo-Ellen, just because she was so helpful, Lourdes and Hailey, and of course, your parents and siblings," Kate replied. "Tell me their names, first and last, and I will add them. Also, any best friends or anyone else you want. I think this first draft should just be our closest people. People we love so much, we can't imagine losing them. Then we can expand it. I'm going to keep it in order so that Rex knows who is a priority. I know that sounds heartless, but we have no idea how many people Rex can, or will, take," Kate explained.

Sinclair was quiet.

"Can I turn on the radio while you think? Or will that be too distracting?" Kate asked.

"Too distracting," Sinclair responded. A minute later, he added, "I don't ever want to live where there are no octopus, koalas, cardinals, Joshua trees, rabbits, or rivers."

"Ha! You know Rex knows we talk like this. He made a list of awesome things when we spoke yesterday. I forgot he said it until just now. I guess all the scary violence talk made me forget. He must listen to us talk. It's so strange." Kate looked up into the sky through the windshield.

"Wow. That is strange. Do you remember what animals or things he mentioned?" Sinclair asked.

"Huh. Let me think," Kate said.

"Wait. Never mind. My point is we say that we don't want to live in cold, quiet, empty space. And I get that the threat of death can change one's mind, but we have no idea what Rex is, where he is, or how he lives. None. Hell, we don't know if the others are good or bad or anything about them. Well, we do know Rex killed hundreds of millions of people! And we do know that space is cold and dark and quiet and airless. Do you really want to go there? Live there?" Sinclair asked, his voice booming.

"Okay. I get what you're saying—it does seem terrible. But like you said, we have no idea what Rex's world is like. It might be okay," Kate hurriedly said, eager to diffuse his anger.

"I think we need a lot more information before we make a decision," Sinclair snapped.

"Well, yes, of course, that would be extremely helpful but Rex never provides enough information about anything," Kate said, becoming exasperated. "But I feel like we should have a list ready. Just in case."

Sinclair scoffed.

Why is he being such a jerk about this? Why is he getting angry?

"I don't. Just putting that into words seems too permanent. If he can hear us, he already knows who is on that list and I think it's premature," Sinclair said.

"Are you angry with me? You sound angry," Kate said.

"Yes, I'm angry, but not with you—with Rex. He needs to give us more information about everything. Now, dammit!" Sinclair smacked the steering wheel with the palm of his hand.

Kate sighed. Getting angry with Sinclair wouldn't help. She needed to calm him down and focus on making the list. *So much for wondering how he controls his emotions.* "I think we need a refined list just in case. What are your parents' names?" Kate asked.

"Nope. I am not adding anyone to that list yet," Sinclair said, shaking his head.

"You *are* angry with me," Kate snapped.

"No. I'm not," Sinclair snapped back.

Kate tossed her phone on the floor. She crossed her arms and looked out the window.

"I need music," Kate announced, turning on the radio. As she scrolled around, a famous old punk song caught her attention. After a few seconds, she started to sing along. Sinclair joined in and they sang together very loudly.

They both sounded angry.

It was going to be a long drive.

FIVE

Sixty Days After the Shooting

The music and angry singing soothed Kate a little.

"I'm sorry. I got angry because you didn't like my list. I guess I didn't think through the repercussions. I mean, what if it's a trap and Rex wants to take some humans with him? Maybe he wants to anally probe us—or eat us," Kate said.

Sinclair laughed. "Rex made hundreds of millions of people shoot themselves at almost the exact same time. He doesn't need our brains or blood or butts. Rex, and the others, don't need anything from us."

"They needed one thing from us," Kate said with a sigh. "They needed us to clean up our mess."

"That's true. We won't even clean up after ourselves to save our own lives. That debris was just as dangerous to astronauts and space tourists as extraterrestrials. I mean, we could claim we didn't know, I guess, at first anyway," Sinclair said.

"But we knew! We know! For decades, people have polluted rivers, lagoons, oceans, hell, our entire water cycle which we totally depend on for life. We pollute our lands and air with deadly chemicals. Plastic is everywhere—killing birds, torturing turtles, and dumping microplastic particles in our blood. We have destroyed our climate with greenhouse gases. We know. Every day, we add more pollution and choose to not clean it up, even though we know it's killing us. NASA knows how deadly all the space debris is. Like Jo-Ellen said, they're playing Russian roulette. Well, they were until we cleaned it up," Kate said.

Her phone rang, startling her out of her dark rant.

"It's Jo-Ellen. Let's see what's up in D.C.," Kate said as she answered and placed it on speaker. She was happy about the distraction. She had grown to really like Jo-Ellen since she helped destroy the space debris. Sinclair and Kate could not have done it without her help. "Hi, Jo-Ellen. I was just thinking of you. How are you?" Kate asked, trying to make her voice sound calm.

"I'm very good. Just enjoying knowing that space is clean and safe. Like before we ever went up there, 1949 pre-Bumper-WAC!" Jo-Ellen laughed. "I spent a few days updating the database. It's perfect now. Well, until the morons at NASA and Space Force and the billionaire space boys fuck it all up again. We need to create a plan to ensure this never happens again. Did you know there was a treaty signed a few years ago by all the nations with space programs that include a provision about space debris? I plan to edit it and see if we can put some real teeth into it. We should start by calling it space pollution and not debris. Debris sounds too innocent. Unfortunately, we will need to deal with the Senate, the laziest and most useless—excuse me, I mean *deliberative*—body in America to get it done. Anyway, I was actually calling to see what you crazy kids are up to."

Sinclair smiled at Kate, seeming to enjoy Jo-Ellen's monologue.

"Wow, you are feeling good. I have never heard you talk so much or so fast before. I like your idea and agree something permanent and meaningful must be done. We have learned so much. We can't just go back to the same old terrible behavior," Kate said.

"Oh, and speaking of databases, the government finally has a complete list of every American that shot themselves on July 14. It took a couple of months because every state had to count, double-check, and submit their data during all the chaos. Hell, it took weeks to deal with all the bodies. Anyway, FEMA is managing it and said in a statement they wanted to be sure it was accurate. The grand total is 70,347,602. I mean, it's not good news, but it needed to be done for the deceased, their families, and posterity," Jo-Ellen said, the giddiness gone from her voice.

"Damn Rex. That is a lot of dead Americans," Kate mumbled, looking up at the sky. She shivered as a cold wave of fear and heartbreak washed over her. *What will Rex and the others do next?* She quickly reached for Sinclair's hand as she remembered him holding Yvette's bloody corpse.

"Where are you?" Jo-Ellen asked.

"Driving to D.C. We plan to drive straight through to get home around midnight. God knows there's no traffic. We're still in Florida," Kate replied. "You're on speaker, by the way."

"Hello, Sinclair. How are you? I assume you are driving?" Jo-Ellen asked.

"Yes. I'm driving and I'm fine. Hey, are you guys still tracking us?" Sinclair asked.

"I'm not. I honestly don't think Space Force is either, but who knows? Since I was working with you at Kennedy Space Center, they won't tell me anything. Right now, everyone just seems so happy about the debris removal; I haven't heard anyone ask about you. Not even about Rex. But now that I think about it, they'll eventually get back to focusing on Rex. At some point, someone will remember Rex caused the mass shooting and that you two know him," Jo-Ellen said.

"I hadn't really thought about that either, but it's inevitable. Especially with so many people knowing we had some help and used new tech. Jack, Otter, Space Force, and NASA staff… they will all wonder what actually happened. There will be questions," Kate said.

"Kate, you should say you were mistaken, and it was just some deranged dude in a cat costume in Rock Creek Park. That would be awesome! What can they do, right? I mean you saved their asses. Just go back to that story," Jo-Ellen said, laughing.

Kate nodded, happy to keep Jo-Ellen on this topic. "I will think about that idea," Kate said. *I hope she does not ask about Rex.*

"Oh, and that reminds me why I was really calling, in addition to seeing how you were doing, of course. Have you heard from Rex?" Jo-Ellen asked.

Kate looked at Sinclair. She did not know what to say. Sinclair shook his head.

"Something went wrong. Rex is not happy," Jo-Ellen murmured. "Your silence is speaking volumes."

Kate hated lying. She thought it was always better to tell the truth. "I saw him yesterday. He said it worked. He told the others we had sent something into space that pulverized the debris. He said they accepted it, that the dangerous debris is gone," Kate replied honestly.

"Okay. That should be great news, so then why the long silence and sad, stressed-out tone? You should be wasted on a beach in Florida, celebrating. You saved the fucking world! But you seem quiet and tense, and you're already driving home. So, something must have gone wrong," Jo-Ellen said.

Kate's shoulders tensed. "I don't want to discuss it on the phone."

"Okay," Jo-Ellen said slowly, sounding disappointed. "Well, now I'm stressed out too."

"We'll call you in the morning," Kate said.

"I'll be at your house in the morning," Jo-Ellen said, just before hanging up.

"We killed her buzz and pissed her off by not elaborating," Sinclair said.

"I know. I feel bad. But if anyone is listening, we could set off a major panic," Kate said, looking out the window and up into the sky.

SIX

Sixty Days After the Shooting

They drove for a few more hours, sometimes listening to music and sometimes the news. Kate would change the station when a newsperson was discussing or doing an interview about the shooting. She could not take any more sadness right now. Her heart needed a break, though she did pause for updates on the virus.

"We should get tested tomorrow. With all the chaos, there were too many times we weren't wearing masks. It'll be a miracle if we don't have COVID," Kate said. It would be just her luck to save the world and then get the coronavirus.

Sinclair shrugged, turning to look at her. "We've been pretty careful. It's a habit now to put on a mask when going indoors or speaking to people outside. We've done well overall. Anyway, I hope we're negative. I like being able to smell."

Ever since I read him the list, we've been out of sorts. I say something and he says the opposite. It's aggravating.

I miss how it used to be when we were consistently on the same page.

"I wonder what Rex would do if we died from COVID? He'd have to work with someone else—maybe Jo-Ellen," Kate mused.

"I'm not sure it would be that simple, that he would just transfer to someone new. He picked you for a reason," Sinclair said.

Okay, here we go again. Whatever I say is wrong.

So much for avoiding shooting fall-out, Kate thought as she quietly scrolled through social media, reading reactions to the newly completed mass shooting victim's database. People were taking screen-shots of the victims' names and writing reasons they loved and missed them. It was too sad and scrolling while in the car was giving her a headache. She wanted to say something to Sinclair about how her list might prevent their loved ones from being added to a death-count database but figured he would shut the conversation down by telling her she was wrong.

Kate angrily twisted the knob on the radio until she hit a station with someone interviewing a high-level NASA scientist. Kate missed the name and only caught a little of the job title.

"Everyone is still celebrating in the space exploration sector, here in the United States and throughout the world. With the debris gone, all of our satellites, research equipment, and astronauts are much safer. Space tourism can take off. I mean, since so much of the risk has been removed, cost is the only controlling factor now," the NASA official said, sounding almost giddy.

"Well, that is great!" the reporter chirped. "The world needed good news and this is fantastic. Now that NASA and the space industry know how to remove space debris, they can just keep making it, right? I mean, if they cause new garbage in order to accomplish their work and obtain their objectives, they can just zap it now?"

Kate felt the anger rise from her toes up to her legs to her torso and settle in her hot, flushed cheeks. The nerve of these people!

Sinclair reached over to turn up the volume.

"It's not garbage; it's debris. Debris is a natural consequence of space exploration. And yes, I am sure they will use the new technology to remove it, when necessary," the NASA official responded confidently.

"He is talking out of his ass! He knows nothing about that technology, and yes, it is garbage," Kate yelled at the radio. Her cheeks throbbed. Her head hurt. Had humanity learned nothing?

"Some critics are saying we should stop producing new debris, knowing how quickly it accumulates and becomes a large, dangerous problem. Is it really a natural consequence or just irresponsible? Shouldn't NASA and others in space be preventing new debris, and if they do create it, clean it up immediately?" the reporter asked.

"Great questions!" Sinclair and Kate said at the same time.

"I wonder if the reporter talked to Jo-Ellen," Kate said. Sinclair nodded.

Kate smiled at him. They were back on the same page.

"I imagine a combination of both. Everyone should be more careful. Like hikers, they should pack it in, pack it out. We've learned so much in the past few decades. For example, urine is recycled on the space station and not ejected into space where it could become a potentially dangerous projectile," the official said.

"Gee, wish you had learned that sooner," Kate said to the radio.

Sinclair placed a calming hand on her knee, giving her a pat before returning his hand to the steering wheel.

"However, when things collide in space, it creates debris. There is so much equipment up there now that some collisions might be inevitable. And some equipment will cease working, thereby becoming debris. Experiments may cause it as well. Space exploration is still so new, mistakes are inevitable if we're going to continue it. We are, after all, only human." The official laughed. "So, the new technology that can pulverize debris into harmless gas will be crucial moving forward."

"What the hell?" Sinclair shouted at the radio. "It does not exist. We don't actually have the technology to do it. That was all Rex! This asshole needs to stop talking. NASA should have come up with a better story and have everyone stick to it. They probably should have said they accidentally destroyed the tech while using it. That should be the official talking point. That way, no one thinks everything is okay now and just returns to the status quo of polluting space.

Letting the public think the miracle technology actually exists is wrong!"

"Now, other nation's space programs and space billionaires will think they can be even less careful because they will assume we can clean up their mess. This is very, very bad," Kate added.

"We need to discuss this with Jo-Ellen tomorrow, maybe NASA and Space Force as well. This bullshit needs to be shut down," Sinclair said.

Kate started turning the knob again but stopped when a voice caught her attention.

"NASA made it seem like only America has the technology, but we don't know. We don't know if it's a Jewish or Chinese space laser or what, but now someone has the power to zap anything they want out of space—just like *that*! It's pure, unbridled power…"

"Geez, I thought most of these conspiracy freaks died in the shooting. That guy wishes someone has that technology! Why does everything have to be so dark and hateful with some people?" Kate snapped off the radio.

They rode in silence for an hour. Neither played with the radio. Kate was still angry at NASA but more relaxed since she and Sinclair seemed copacetic again.

"Kate, I was thinking about that database Jo-Ellen was talking about. The FEMA one. Would you do me a favor and see if Theo Mast is in it?" Sinclair asked.

Kate's heart raced. She had planned to look up her middle school nemesis, the boy she thought intended to shoot up their school, several times since the global mass shooting. If he'd had access to guns as a teen, it was very likely he had one or more as an adult. But she always got distracted before doing the research.

"Aren't you curious?" Sinclair asked quietly, seeming to sense Kate's anxiousness. "Only do it if you want to."

Memories flooded Kate's mind of her reporting the bag with the huge gun, maybe multiple guns. The police, some classmates, and Theo Mast had twisted the situation and blamed Kate. She recalled her and her mom leaving Colorado forever to get away from the infuriating quagmire.

Oh well, she liked hot Florida way better than cold and snowy Colorado.

"Yes. Okay. I want to know," Kate said as she did a search on her phone. When she found the database, she typed in Theodore Mast, Colorado. His name popped up.

Wow. Kate wasn't sure how to feel. *On the one hand, any death was sad. Maybe he had gotten help and was a better person. But what if he had held onto the urge to scare and hurt people after all these years?*

"He was still living in the same town, and he did shoot and kill himself on the 14th, according to this database," Kate said quietly.

Sinclair reached over and gently squeezed her knee. "You okay?"

"I hope he didn't spend these past fifteen years terrorizing and lying to people. I hope he learned his lesson when we were in school and was not an asshole the rest of his life," Kate said, shuddering as dark thoughts crossed her mind. She could still see his face, like it just happened, as he threatened to kill her and her mom while clutching a bag with at least one large gun in it.

I'm happy he's dead. Thanks, Rex.

Sinclair released her knee and took Kate's hand.

"I wish I could have done more to shut him down," Kate said, wiping angry tears away.

"Kate, you were just a kid. Looks like there was some karma in the end," Sinclair said as he kissed her balled-up fist.

"Now, would you please look up Yvette?" Sinclair asked. "I want to know that she was included."

Kate looked at Sinclair, but he was staring out the window, focused on the road ahead. She typed *Yvette Jones, Washington D.C.* into the database.

"Yes, she is here. I'm so sorry, Sinclair." Kate took his hand and squeezed it against her chest.

"It's okay, Kate. I guess it's official now. We knew Rex killed her. We know why. It's just a database. But she was a person, a person I loved a whole lot at one time," he said.

Rex killed so many people, Kate thought. Some of them, like Theo, probably deserved it. Some were rapists, serial killers, trophy hunters, trappers, child molesters, gangbangers—people that hurt others for fun and pleasure and deserved to die. But most of them were not bad people and did not deserve to die.

Kate began typing an idea into her phone. "I think I'll call it the Ark, rather than the list. Sounds more positive."

"Huh. Interesting. Are you going to match everyone up? The same number of males and females like the biblical Ark?" Sinclair asked.

"Way to be so binary," Kate said, flashing him a smile. "We have no idea if gender means anything in Rex's world anyway. Please give me your parents' names. Please give me all your loved ones' names. You heard that NASA asshole. We didn't learn anything. There could be new debris being created right now. Rex and the others will know. Let's be safe and create the list, whoops, I mean the Ark," Kate said.

Sinclair bit his lip. "What if I give you my parents' names and Rex takes them and they are devastated that their siblings were not included? Or other people they love? They might be consumed by guilt. What if they hate space and are angry that they are up there? What if they are angry that we just made this huge decision for them?" Sinclair asked. "What if they don't survive the transport up? My parents are old and not very healthy. Will they need their meds up there?"

"They won't be dead. That is the only thing we can promise them. I think you are overthinking this. Alive and safe up there, or most likely dead down here," Kate said, getting angry again. "Rex killed 70,347,602 Americans on July 14! What will the others do next?"

"I don't think you are thinking enough! Neither of us wants to live in space, but we are considering bringing people up there without their consent!" Sinclair said, sounding frustrated and angry. "I think you are being impetuous. Sometimes I forget how young you are."

"So, this is now an age thing? Millennial vs Xer? I am so tired of generational battles," Kate snapped.

"Huh, I thought you were a Zoomer," Sinclair said, glancing at her. "And I'm not an Xer. I'm an elder millennial and I'm used to being insulted about my generation and I hate it, so I apologize. That was a cheap shot. You are not immature, actually one of the most mature twenty-somethings I have ever met."

"I'm twenty-seven. A late millennial," Kate said, hoping he would tell her his age.

Kate waited for him to volunteer it, when he didn't, she just asked. "How old are you?"

"Thirty-nine. Way older than you. I have a lot more life experience and that is why I'm very worried about this list. And though you are not immature, regarding this matter, I think you are being a little selfish," Sinclair said.

Kate gasped as her face flushed with heat. She reached into the back seat and grabbed a bag of pretzels. She ripped it open and started eating. She thought maybe she was getting hangry because she was very angry with Sinclair.

Why is he being so obstinate about the Ark? I'm not being selfish! I want to save lives!

"I need to take a piss. I haven't seen a car in a while so I'm just going to pull over," Sinclair said as he slowed the car and stopped on the shoulder. He slammed the car door as he got out and stomped toward the edge of the woods.

Kate got out to stretch her legs and quickly walked around the car a couple of times while eating pretzels. She leaned on the hood of the car and shouted so Sinclair could hear her from where he was standing. "You know we could die today! These could be our last few minutes alive. If we have a list and suddenly everyone is puking in the white room, they might just be relieved to be alive!" Kate shoved a handful of pretzels into her mouth.

"I know we have been spending an extraordinary amount of time together, but let's please have some boundaries. We can discuss this in the car," Sinclair shouted over his shoulder.

Kate leaned back and smiled, realizing her conversation might be preventing Sinclair from peeing. Then the thought of frozen pee floating through space crossed her mind and made her sad. She shoved more pretzels in her mouth and jumped when a police car quietly pulled up behind Sinclair's car.

It seemed to come out of nowhere. Kate was so startled that she choked on the pretzels. She bent at the waist, coughing.

Two police officers got quickly out of the car. "Everything all right here?" one asked, sounding concerned.

"We're fine," Kate croaked. "You startled me and made me choke on a pretzel."

The cops just stared at her and then at Sinclair.

"Just taking a bathroom break and stretching our legs. It's safer here, outside, due to the virus," Kate said.

It's usually illegal to urinate outside, but does that include the side of a highway? This is strange. Why did they stop?

"Uh-huh," one of the officers said.

Sinclair finished and walked quickly over to Kate. She pulled a hand sanitizer from her pocket and handed it to Sinclair.

"Can we see your IDs?" one of the officers asked. He had a trendy 5 o'clock shadow beard.

"What? Why? We haven't done anything wrong. You didn't even pull us over," Kate said.

"We are just concerned. We want to make sure everything is okay. Your identification please," the clean-shaven officer said.

Sinclair pulled his wallet out of his back pocket and slid out his driver's license, handing it to the officer.

Kate did not even have one, so she just kept eating pretzels.

"I can understand why a woman leaning on a car eating pretzels while watching her friend pee would raise your concern," Kate said sarcastically.

The bearded cop got back in the patrol car, presumably to run a check on Sinclair's license.

"I can't believe this is actually happening," Kate said, her mouth full. She offered a pretzel to Sinclair.

"I can," Sinclair said, rejecting the offer of pretzels. "It's been happening my whole life."

Kate swallowed hard, both on the pretzels and her white privilege.

"Okay. Everything checks out. We just needed to be sure," the bearded cop said when he returned, handing the license back to Sinclair.

"I thought most of the racist cops had died. This makes me really sad. We were not doing a thing to raise your concern. We certainly didn't break any laws. Why did you stop?" Kate asked.

"We aren't racist," the clean-shaven cop said, sounding defensive. He puffed up like he wanted to start something.

"People are acting strange and we're being extra careful," the bearded cop said apologetically.

"Because of the pandemic and mass shooting and all the sadness and death? Yes, we should all be kinder to each other, not suspicious," Kate snapped.

"Of course, I agree, but with all the alien invasion talk, people are on edge again. Doing strange things. I'm sure it's just a story, but after the shooting, people are scared and willing to believe anything. Anyway, safe travels," the nicer officer said, turning to return to their idling car.

"An alien invasion?" Kate and Sinclair said in unison.

Had the next round of violence begun? And if so, where?

SEVEN

Sixty Days After the Shooting

What did the cops mean by 'alien invasion talk'? *This news makes the Ark all the more important.*

Back on the highway, Kate turned the knob on the radio, checked social media, and texted Jo-Ellen to see if some new bizarre or violent event had happened. So far, things seemed the same, but there was a lot of speculation about the debris removal.

"I just think saving people we love is important, Sinclair. They'll forgive us if they don't like the situation. They'll know we did it out of love." Kate sighed. They had been debating and speculating on the alien invasion comment for hours and Kate had a headache. "And if there really is talk about an alien invasion, I'm not sure they'll be as shocked as you think if they end up in the white room."

"Yes, you're right. They might not be shocked. Bizarre things do keep happening. But think of their anguish and guilt about the people they love that are left behind. We'll feel it too. What about their pets? If all humans die, nature will rebound and thrive, but it will be very difficult for many animals. What if the people you pick resent you? They will see you as the leader because of your relationship with Rex. Whatever feelings they feel—be it guilt, remorse, relief, or love—those feelings will be directed at you. You will take the brunt of it all," Sinclair said passionately as he stared into her eyes.

"Keep your eyes on the road," Kate snapped petulantly. She knew he was right to bring up all these issues, but she was tired of arguing.

The drive was taking forever. She wished Rex could send them home at warp speed.

"I mean, if extraterrestrials exist why can't warp speed?" Kate mumbled to herself.

She turned the knob on the radio, but there was still no discussion of an alien invasion.

"Not to generation bash, but you are the only person under fifty who listens to the radio," Sinclair quipped.

"I like the radio on road trips," Kate said. "It reminds me of traveling with my mom. We didn't always agree on music, but we could both listen to NPR or take a chance on a radio station if the DJ was choosing the songs for us. We both liked to be exposed to new things: music, ideas, and people talking about their lives."

Sinclair smiled and nodded his head at her explanation.

"But that makes me think about people talking about their lives and jobs. I wonder who said what to who? I mean like, what, thirty NASA staff knew something strange was up, right? They were probably wondering why we were in the observation room watching the debris being pulverized. At least, what, twenty at Space Force between the interrogation at HQ in D.C., and the staff at Kennedy? Another maybe ten or so on Jack's team—sure, they were mostly security people, but they must have known something strange was happening. And us rushing to add equipment to a satellite launch at the last second. That had to raise suspicion among that flight team. Add our family and friends, oh, and Otter and his team. That is a lot of people," Kate said. "Someone must have told someone and now it's on the internet. I hope *we* are the alien invasion the cop mentioned."

"When almost one hundred people know something curious, it's destined to get out. I guess the first few days were a relief for all involved, but now that the news is leaking, people might be confused and scared. It seems to be spreading fast. I mean, if two highway cops are talking about it, it's out in public," Sinclair said.

"I just want to get home and crawl into my own bed. I want to shower with my products and put on my own clean clothes," Kate said, dramatically stretching her arms overhead. "I don't care that the world is confused and scared. However, I do want to finish the Ark so I can sleep soundly."

"Well, I'm eager to get home and sleep in my bed and maybe not have a list ready until I feel confident it's the right thing to do. Or at least the best thing, or maybe just the better option," Sinclair responded.

They continued to bicker about the Ark until they crossed the 14th Street bridge into D.C.

"I always forget how beautiful D.C. is. Every time I enter this city, it takes my breath away. The Washington Monument, Lincoln Memorial, and Kennedy Center are all lit up, like a big 'Welcome to D.C.' sign. It looks so hopeful. Of course, there is a lot of trash, stupidity, manipulation, hate, racism, sexism, misogyny, corporate abuse, greed, and selfishness, but I still love this city," Kate murmured.

Sinclair reached for Kate's hand. He held it, squeezed it, and kissed it. "I feel the same. We need to save it and the people that live here."

Kate felt a wave of heat. They had not touched for several hours because of the arguing, and now Kate realized how much she missed it.

"We are D.C. residents trying to save the world, and we don't even have a Senator to discuss this crisis with if we wanted to. We would have to beg for the attention of someone from another state, and they always say, 'I only listen to constituents.' It's total bullshit and really unfair. No taxation without representation, except here. It's so fucking racist," Kate said, flushing red with anger at her rare use of the f-word. She was tired from the long drive, yet her heart was racing because she was holding Sinclair's hand.

"Wow, you swore, and the f-word at that," Sinclair said with a little laugh.

"I feel passionate about D.C. statehood," Kate replied, feeling a little embarrassed by her intense emotions.

"We will be home in ten minutes. Kyle will be happy to see you," Sinclair said quietly.

Kate dropped Sinclair's hand, suddenly feeling guilty. "Kyle! What am I going to say to Kyle?" Kate asked.

Sinclair took a deep breath. "My advice? Nothing tonight. It's after one. Tell him you're too tired to go into everything."

"Seriously. That's true. I'm so tired. And I don't even know where to start," Kate said.

Sinclair turned down their street. Kate was thrilled to see her house. She was eager to get out of the car but not eager at all to leave Sinclair's side. She felt anxious and sad to be leaving him.

What does that mean?

EIGHT

Sixty-One Days After the Shooting

Kate opened the front door quietly. She put her bag on the floor and went into the kitchen to fill her water bottle. She crept up the stairs, hoping she would not wake up Kyle.

As she entered the bedroom, Kyle shot straight up in bed. "Who's there?"

Kate jumped. "Me, geez, Kyle, you scared me!"

"Kate? You're home!" Kyle leaped out of bed and pulling her into a tight embrace. "I'm so happy you are home! And safe! Ha! Almost had a heart attack when I saw you in the doorway. Seriously, I almost pissed myself–I was that startled." He laughed. "You've been gone so long. Aside from Amanda, no one has been here since you left."

Kate figured she must be very tired because Kyle's hug just felt clingy and possessive.

"Sorry, babe. I am exhausted and I didn't want to disturb you so I was trying to be quiet." Kate wondered how many times Amanda had come over.

Kyle abruptly pulled out of the hug and snapped on the lamp.

"Okay, tell me everything. You checked in often to say you were safe but never with many details. You drove to Florida to track down Rex, and it must have worked. Right? You found Rex and destroyed the debris? I've seen stuff on the news and online. I never saw mention of you or Sinclair, but I think I put it together. Am I right? Never mind, you tell me. What happened? You were gone for almost two weeks! Where did you go? What did you do?" Kyle asked in a rush.

She wasn't going to get out of having this conversation now. Kate sat down on the bed.

"Okay, I am going to tell you the whole story from the beginning, but first you need to promise not to tell anyone else, ever. This is going to sound crazy. Most of it is really unbelievable, but it's all true. I need you to not ask questions or interrupt me until I am finished, okay? I will tell the story then we'll go to bed. We can talk more tomorrow. Is that okay?" Kate yawned.

Kyle nodded enthusiastically.

As Kate collected her thoughts, she realized she had not told Kyle what Rex really was or about the white room. So, she started from the beginning, the first run in Rock Creek when the shooting happened. She told him about the second run when Rex pulled her into the white room. She explained that Rex changed forms but settled in as a large orange cat that looked like Rex, their old foster cat, so that's what she called him. She told Kyle how Rex wanted her to tell Space Force and NASA that they must remove the dangerous debris within five days. She explained the loopholes she tried to exploit with Sinclair's help.

"I thought telling my boss covered me telling Space Force and telling Sinclair would cover telling NASA. The loopholes didn't really work, but they bought the world time," Kate said, laying down on the bed and kicking off her shoes.

"So, the harasser in the park was really an extraterrestrial of some type," Kate continued with a another yawn. "Anyway, Space Force was stalking me and kind of found out because Jo-Ellen was eavesdropping, and as you know, I was interviewed at Space Force. I told them the entire truth. I told them about Rex's warnings. I told them they had to remove the debris and pollution and make space safe. But no, they decided to frame me and tell the world I was a person of interest in the mass shooting. You know how that went. You saved me from that angry mob." Kate paused and looked at Kyle.

Kyle nodded; his brow furrowed in concern.

"Sinclair had been doing research into Yvette's work. She knew about a huge collision that happened a year ago. He thought it might have something to do with the debris Rex was so bothered by. So, we talked to some of Yvette's colleagues and found out the debris was stored in Florida at Kennedy Space Center. Well, most of it anyway." Kate paused, sitting up to take a big swig of water from her bottle.

"There was so much craziness. Police threatened Sinclair. Scheming with Jo-Ellen and her contacts. Anyway, we came up with a plan and, with Rex's help, pulverized all the space debris, but made it look like us Earthlings did it to appease Rex's bosses." Kate paused for more water, then backtracked and explained about the white room and how Rex pulled her—and once, Sinclair—into the otherworldly space.

"It was so cool watching the satellite get launched with our special equipment. It was so exciting watching space being cleaned up. No matter what happens, we made space safer for everyone. Well, for now."

Should I say more? The situation isn't over. Kyle deserves to know that. He's a good guy. And he loves me.

"Anyway, I thought it had worked—we all thought it worked—but it might not have, and we, what's left of the human race, might still be in danger," Kate said, her eyes drooping shut. It felt so good to close her eyes. It felt so comforting to be in her bed, even if she missed Sinclair's steady presence. "That's pretty much it."

"Wow. I'm not sure what to think. Does Sinclair believe this story?" Kyle asked, his brow furrowed.

Kate's eyes snapped open. "What do you mean? Of course, Sinclair believes it. He was with me the entire time."

"You both went up into a white spaceship and spoke to a giant cat that caused the mass shooting? Both of you together?" Kyle asked.

"Rex, the cat, is some kind of avatar, as I said. And the white room may or may not be a part of the ship. I don't know," Kate said, curling up, eager to fall asleep.

"Not so fast, Kate." Kyle grabbed her shoulder and jostled her. "I've been here at home while you're running around with our neighbor. It's my turn to ask questions. I have so many questions."

Kate was angered by Kyle's tone. *He seems completely incredulous, as I predicted. Why would I make this up?*

Kate ignored Kyle's pestering and fell asleep in the same clothes she had worn all day.

NINE

Sixty-One Days After the Shooting

Kate woke up alone. Rubbing the sleep out of her eyes, she stretched her arms overhead and heard a loud clang from the kitchen.

Kyle must be making breakfast.

She slept heavily despite numerous nightmares. In one, her mother was in the white room yelling at Kate for leaving baby Katniss behind. In another, several people were floating around the white room, occasionally vomiting. Despite the retching, no one spoke.

Dammit. Sinclair's concerns are penetrating my subconscious!

After a glorious shower with all of her favorite products, Kate stumbled down to the kitchen, where Kyle handed her a cup of coffee, kissed her cheek, and indicated she should sit down. A few seconds later, he gave her avocado toast and a bowl of fruit.

"Thanks! This looks delicious. I'm so happy to be home, babe." Kate dug in.

"I'm so happy you're home, Kate," Kyle said, but he didn't sound happy. Instead, his words matched his furrowed brow.

"What's wrong?" Kate asked with alarm. "Has something happened?"

"Kate, you were tired and a little delirious last night. I'm not sure what happened in Florida, but I do know that it did not include extraterrestrials. I've read the alien conspiracy stories online. Even mainstream news outlets are discussing them. Is that where you got this crazy idea to blame everything on a giant cat?" Kyle asked, sounding concerned.

He didn't believe her. She'd kept him in the dark to protect him, but now he thought she was certifiable. She clenched and unclenched her fist. "My first meeting with Rex was in Rock Creek Park, not Florida. I didn't tell you at the time because I was afraid that you would think I was crazy. Which you obviously do. Then I didn't tell you because I was trying to protect you. This all started before any space invasion rumors or internet conspiracies were spread. And now that I think about it, they aren't crazy conspiracies. At least some of it is true."

Why doesn't Kyle, of all people, believe me? My mother believed me. Sinclair and Jo-Ellen gave me the benefit of the doubt. Why can't my boyfriend do the same?

Kate reached out for his hand but Kyle pulled it back.

"Does *Sinclair* believe you?" Kyle asked again, with mocking emphasis on Sinclair's name.

Kate's cheeks grew red. "Yes, of course he does. He has been involved since the beginning. If you need a witness or someone to verify my account of what's happened, he is it. Though I am kind of upset that you don't believe me. I know it sounds crazy, but why on Earth would I make this up?"

Kyle paced back and forth. "You want me to believe that a large cat space alien named Rex caused the mass shooting because he was angry about debris in space? And, of all the people on the planet, this big cat alien reached out to you because you had contacts at Space Force and NASA? And you tried to trick him, this mass murderer? And it sort of worked. But then he, the mass murderer, got in on the crazy charade with you and Sinclair. You guys all worked together and tricked the world? Oh, but whoopsie, it only tricked humans, I mean Earthlings, right? Not the other extraterrestrials? This whole story is insane," Kyle said, throwing up his hands.

"I know it sounds unreal, but I'm not lying. We are still in a crisis. I really need you to believe me—to trust me, Kyle," Kate said, as tears of frustration filled her eyes.

"Right, like you trusted me when you said a mentally unwell man—not an alien cat— harassed you in the park. Or when you said you were heading to New York to find him after I risked my life so you could get to safety. Or all the times we spoke on the phone and you never mentioned aliens or being snatched up into space?" Kyle asked, almost shouting.

Kyle is right to be suspicious. I have been lying to him. How am I going to explain why I did it without hurting him? How do I tell Kyle I didn't trust him, but I expect him to trust me now?

"Honestly, Kate, I have no idea if you're lying now or you were then. Actually, I'm pretty sure you are lying now because this is fucking crazy!" Kyle slammed his fist down on the table, shaking her coffee mug. Coffee sloshed on the tabletop.

"Knock, knock," called Jo-Ellen as she opened the front door and walked into the kitchen. She wore a Space Force mask and carried a travel mug of coffee. Kate recognized it as one of Sinclair's. *She must have gone there first*, Kate thought, as she looked around for a mask.

Sinclair followed behind her, not looking at Kate. "Everything okay?" Sinclair asked Kyle.

"We could hear you shouting from the porch," Jo-Ellen added, increasing the awkward tension.

"Maybe you could come back later. We're in the middle of something," Kyle said. "Kate just got back home and we have a lot to discuss."

"Oh no, we don't have time for that," Jo-Ellen said, getting straight to business. "Kyle, everything Kate said is true. Sinclair filled me in a little on the current situation, but I have questions for Kate that need answers now. If the others are about to punish us, we need to strategize on how to prevent that from happening."

Kate was lost in thought, wallowing in Kyle's anger and the lies she had told to protect him.

"Hello, earth to Kate." Jo-Ellen snapped her fingers.

"What?" Kate said, realizing she missed something.

"Tell me exactly what Rex said, starting with the Ark."

TEN

Sixty-One Days After the Shooting

"I can do better than that," Kate said, rummaging through the bag she had borrowed from her mom. She pulled out the slightly crumpled list, the one she had made following her last encounter with Rex.

"Here you go," Kate said, handing it to Sinclair. "Read it out loud."

Sinclair looked at the list. "Are you sure, Kate?" Sinclair asked. "This is heavy stuff."

There was a knock on the front door and everyone turned to it.

"I'll get it," Kyle said.

"Kate, do you want Kyle to know about this? Did you really tell him everything? I only ask because you expressed concern before," Sinclair hissed.

She'd never seen Kyle so angry. But she still trusted him. "I told him everything else. Might as well tell him this, I guess. He is my boyfriend. We should trust each other."

"We heard him shouting. Is everything okay?" Sinclair asked.

"I appreciate your concern, Sinclair. I really do. I think it was just a lot for him to hear and he needs time to process it. Though I do wish he would have believed me without needing you two to confirm the story. I'm not sure he totally believes it now. But I didn't trust him before and he knows that, so, yes, he is angry," Kate said.

How am I going to fix things with Kyle, with Sinclair and Jo-Ellen here? But really, we should be focused on the Ark and saving people from violence right now. It's much more important than soothing Kyle.

Kate rubbed her face. Tears of frustration welled up in her eyes for the second time since she entered the kitchen.

Jo-Ellen's gaze went from Kate to Sinclair as they spoke. "Well, where did he go? If you want him involved, he should be here."

Kate looked toward the front door, which Kyle had gone to answer, but he was gone. She had been distracted by Sinclair's questions and didn't notice he'd slipped out. She stepped outside to find Kyle leaning on the porch railing, speaking to a young police officer. The cop was in full uniform, except she did not appear to have a gun. Nor did she have on a mask. The cop glanced over at Kate and smiled.

"Hi, Kate. Welcome home," she said.

Kate was stunned into silence. She was one of the most beautiful women Kate had ever seen.

"Kate, this is Amanda. The police officer that I have been working with to keep our street safe since the mob attacked us. I told you about her," Kyle said.

Well, Kyle, you did not tell me that Amanda was stunning, with perfect cheekbones, a big smile, bright white teeth, and amazing eyes. You must have forgot to mention all of that.

Kate was about to stammer something when Amanda cut in. "We are happy you are home and safe after your amazing adventure. Kyle was just filling me in. I suspected that something more was up, but wow, extraterrestrials *and* world-saving? It all seems so incredible—almost unbelievable."

What the hell! Did he tell Amanda? He just came out here and told this gorgeous woman my story, the one that he said he does not actually believe? The story I told him not to tell anyone! Oh my God, I'd been right all along. I shouldn't have told him anything!

"Well, I guess I should thank you for protecting the neighborhood and working with Kyle. That mob was terrifying. And, I can't emphasize this enough, please do not repeat anything Kyle said or we could end up with more pissed off crowds," Kate said, trying not to show her anger.

"Kate, Amanda won't say anything. She hasn't before. I totally trust her," Kyle said, smiling at Amanda.

Dammit, Kyle! She didn't really know anything before you, idiot. I only just told you the full story and she might feel an obligation to report it!

"Well, okay, but please keep this all on the down-low, you know, moving forward. It's over and the debris was removed and we saved the world and NASA and Space Force are happy, so no reason to discuss it further," Kate said.

"But Kyle said you're still in crisis mode. What does that mean? Are people still in danger? From your alien friend?" Amanda asked.

"Ha, ha, no. That was a misunderstanding, I think. We have guests I need to get back to. It was a pleasure meeting you, Amanda. And again, thanks for all your help while I was away," Kate said, walking back inside and shutting the door.

Kate stood with her back to the door for a minute, taking deep breaths. She put her hands over her mask-covered mouth.

What the hell?! Did he really tell Amanda what I said? Who knows if he even got it right since, until Sinclair and Jo-Ellen arrived, he didn't even believe me! Well, I hope he presented it to Amanda as too crazy to be true. Kate ran her fingers through her tangled hair. *I wish I had put on make-up and proper clothes before coming downstairs. I must look like a terrible mess.*

"Everything okay, Kate?" Sinclair asked, walking toward her. "Come here," he said, pulling her in for a hug.

"Let me get a few things. We need to get out of here. We can't work here," Kate whispered into his ear. "We can't let Kyle know anything else."

ELEVEN

Sixty-One Days After the Shooting

An hour later, Sinclair, Jo-Ellen, and Kate were sitting in Jo-Ellen's small apartment in a hip part of D.C., poring over Kate's notes from her most recent encounter with Rex.

"Okay, I will read the list out loud," Jo-Ellen said.

1. Rex told the others the debris was pulverized—but they are coming anyway.

2. Rex does not know if our ploy worked.

3. They are concerned Rex has been here too long.

4. The important VIPs that died were his parents.

5. He showed me what they saw: the debris, the pee, the collision, the explosion, the ejection.

6. He doesn't know what they plan to do to us or to Earth when they arrive.

7. Rex said to get Sinclair, mom, and whomever else I value so that Rex can bring them up before the violence starts.

8. They are coming fast, soon (maybe five days—my guess, not Rex's words).

"I have so many questions. His parents were killed by the debris? Who are these others and why do they have power over Rex? Are they like, his supervisors? The extraterrestrials have so much power; hell, Rex made hundreds of millions of people shoot themselves at practically the same time, but they couldn't make their ship avoid a little debris? None of this makes any sense!" Jo-Ellen said, her voice getting louder as she spoke.

"Are you angry? With who? Rex?" Kate asked.

"I think a clue is that they were worried he was here a long time. Maybe the mass shooting was not as easy as it would appear. Why was Rex here—out there—for such a long time? And why are the others worried about it?" Sinclair asked.

"Okay, we need to focus on the right things," Kate said, standing up and pacing. "We're focusing on the wrong things, like Rex and the others. We can't control them. We need to finalize the list, or Ark, of people we want Rex to save. We need that ready first as we have no idea when the others will rain down their wrath. Let's create the list and get it to Rex, somehow, and then we can try to untangle everything else."

Kate walked over to a huge window that overlooked what would normally be a very busy D.C. crosstown road. The office buildings and shops were still under a mandatory shutdown. The sad and dystopian view suited Kate's mood.

I wish I was back in Florida. The stress was easier to bear near palm trees, the lagoon, and the beach. I thought it would be nice to be home, but Kyle is not being helpful and obviously has a crush on Amanda. It's probably why he is telling her everything. I doubt he would keep an old male cop in the loop.

"I'm with Sinclair on that. So, let's move on," Jo-Ellen said, interrupting Kate's brooding.

"What?" Kate asked.

"We can't make a list. We have no idea what the conditions will be like in space. We don't know if Rex is good or bad, and the mass shooting makes me lean toward bad, really bad. We need to come up with a plan to stop the others. Making a list is just giving up," Jo-Ellen said.

"Okay, so you are not on the list," Kate said, picking up her phone. "Are you sure? I will delete both of your names if that's what you want. I wish you would reconsider, but of course, it's your life," Kate said.

"Who else is on the list?" Jo-Ellen asked.

Kate read her the shortlist, to which she had added a few more friends. "Removing Sinclair, and his family, reduced it quite a lot." She squeezed her eyes shut and continued. "I picture myself in the white room trying to explain what happened to the people on the list. If the conversation in my mind seems authentic and includes hugs, I leave the name on it. Sinclair was right when he said some of them may never forgive me or may even hate me for taking them into space. I only included the people I love so much that I think I could handle their hate."

Everyone was quiet for a minute.

"Put me back on the list," Jo-Ellen said. "Just in case."

TWELVE

Sixty-One Days After the Shooting

A loud bang on the door made Kate jump.

"What the hell?" Jo-Ellen asked loudly, heading to the door. She looked through the peephole. "It's the police. Looks like there's a few of them. Amanda has been busy."

"Dammit, Kyle! I never should have told him. I know he is just trying to be helpful, but this is not helpful at all. We don't have time for this!" Kate said, squeezing her fists into tight balls.

Jo-Ellen opened the door with a big smile plastered on her face. "Hello, officers. What can I do for you? And let me just note, this is a private residence, and you may not enter without a warrant."

"We have arrest warrants for you, Jo-Ellen Marshall, Kate Stellute, and Sinclair Jones," a police officer announced as he strolled into the apartment. "Please mask up."

More young cops followed him in. They seemed too young to have graduated from the police academy. One started to read their Miranda rights, as the other officers approached them with handcuffs. "You have the right to remain silent. Anything you say can and will be used against you in a court of law. You have a right to an attorney…"

Kate was not listening. As the plastic handcuffs were pulled tight on her wrists, she grumbled, "I'm going to kill Kyle for this. What was he thinking?"

"Hush, Kate. You're not going to kill anyone. You're upset. The cop just told you: you have the right to remain silent and you really should," Sinclair said, laughing a little. "Plus, we have not broken any laws and will quickly be released."

"That's what they all say," a cop that looked sixteen huffed, guiding Sinclair out the door.

The cop holding Kate's arm led her out of the apartment. "Causing a mass shooting, or covering up the cause of a mass shooting, is definitely a crime," he muttered.

Again, I'm being blamed by the police for something I didn't do!

"Geez, this is a little overkill," Kate said as she walked out of the apartment building and saw several police cars waiting for them.

The cop guided her into the back seat, then stood outside the car for several minutes. Kate watched as Sinclair and Jo-Ellen were put in two different cars.

Why are we being separated? I hate the idea of being apart from Sinclair. How did Kyle's baby cop, as he referred to her when we spoke on the phone when I was heading down to Florida, get three arrest warrants in an hour? She must have been waiting for us to return from Florida. Amanda said she suspected something more was up; I bet she had this all greased and ready to go.

While a cop she'd never seen before slid into the driver's side, the one who had handcuffed her, and accused her of being involved in the mass shooting, got into the passenger seat.

The makings of a panic attack washed over Kate as she watched the vehicle with Sinclair inside drive away. *Deep breaths. Count to five. I need to stay calm.*

"Where are they taking Sinclair and Jo-Ellen?" Kate asked.

"Same place as you—to the warehouse. They'll process you there," the driver replied.

"We're all going to the same place? In three separate cars? No wonder we have a climate crisis," Kate snapped, taking her frustration out on the cops. "This seems very wasteful."

The driver looked at Kate in the rearview mirror but did not say anything.

"I sure hope you reuse these plastic cuffs as well. Single-use plastic should be illegal," Kate added. "And wasn't the police force dramatically reduced in size? I sure hope no serious crimes happen while wasting police resources on us." Her anxiety was making her angry.

"Crime has been seriously reduced in D.C.," the driver said.

She looked out the window as they drove along. When they passed a police precinct office along the way, she asked, "What is the warehouse? Is that another word for jailhouse?"

"It's a big warehouse near the Capitol. Capitol Hill police process arrests for protests there. And, I guess, sometimes metropolitan police." The driver replied without meeting her eyes in the rearview mirror.

"Why are we going there and not a regular precinct or jail?" Kate asked.

"I have no idea," the cop in the passenger seat snarled. "Though, most precinct offices have been closed due to the massive loss of police lives on July 14. If I had not been on a hike with my kids and he had not been on a run, we would be dead."

He definitely thinks I did it.

And how terribly sad. They both must have survivor's remorse and PTSD. They are so brave for continuing with their jobs. Of course, they are safer now, with fewer criminals and guns, but I should stop giving them a hard time. I wonder if they had been in a fugue state, like many gun owners that could not get to their guns within the fifteen minutes. Interesting that exercise kind of saved their lives. I wonder if they've thought about that.

As they drove past a huge empty car inspection station, and into a parking lot, Kate saw dozens of black SUVs and police cruisers.

"What the hell is going on here?" the driver asked his partner.

"Well, now we know why they wanted us to bring her to the warehouse. Lots of VIPs, from the look of things." The cop in the passenger seat straightened his hat. "This must be for her. She knows about the mass shooting and might know a space alien."

"Is that a Ferrari?" the driver wondered as he pulled up alongside it.

Both cops got out of the squad car and slowly circled the sports car. Kate could see their mouths moving as they spoke to each other, but she couldn't hear the words. After they thoroughly inspected the car, they collected Kate and walked her into the warehouse.

Kate scanned the crowded room; it was a huge warehouse with garage doors large enough to drive a truck through. It reminded her of the hangar with the debris at Kennedy Space Center, albeit not as large. Tables and desks lined the walls, and there were dozens of metal folding chairs scattered about. It seemed like there were four quadrants to the room with impossibly tall stacks of boxes, folded tables, chairs, and hundreds of cases of plastic water bottles lining the walls. In the center of the room were dozens of people, most with their backs to Kate. She was taking this all in as she searched for Sinclair. Her heart jumped when she spotted him sitting beside a desk on the other side of the room. When he noticed her, their eyes locked, and he gave her a reassuring nod.

Thank the gods he's okay.

As she was being led to another desk, one of the huge warehouse doors opened and Jo-Ellen was guided into the room.

"Don't let them speak to each other. Not a single word," an older cop in full dress bellowed from across the room. "Keep them separated."

Kate considered shouting, "Hello, Sinclair," just to freak them out. She laughed at the thought but refrained. She felt a giddy rush seeing that Sinclair was okay and figured she was amped up on adrenalin. She had never been arrested before.

Kate was taken to a desk on the opposite side of the room from where Sinclair was sitting. Jo-Ellen was somewhere behind her.

"We are going to process your arrest here and then you will be interviewed," a new cop said to Kate. He had to speak loudly to be heard over the other officers' conversations.

"Process away but I'm not speaking a word without an attorney," Kate replied.

"Of course, that's my Ferrari! Think any of these government stiffs could afford that beauty. No way in hell," Jack's surfer boy voice broke through the din. "It's a hybrid so it gets pretty good gas mileage, you know, to offset the $4 million price tag!" He laughed loudly at his own joke.

So, this is not a real arrest, or at least not a normal one, Kate thought as she looked over her shoulder. Many of the people were Space Force and NASA staff. She recognized Tonya and Malcolm and the acting general whose name she couldn't remember. Jack was here and she thought she recognized the cattle king guy, who was launching the satellite they hitched a ride on.

"Is this like pretend processing? This can't be a normal arrest with all these people here. I mean, unless they were arrested for protesting something?" Kate asked the cop as he focused on his computer's screen. "Certainly not for climate change or the environment. Not this crowd. Maybe they were demanding more tax breaks for rich, White men? You know, so they can really start the space tourism industry." Kate's voice dripped with sarcasm.

The cop wordlessly glanced at Kate but just kept typing.

Kate sighed loudly. *This arrest is totally bogus. I'm not saying another word to anyone, as Sinclair advised.*

"It's not a regular arrest, or the mayor and attorney general wouldn't be here. This is highly unusual. But they told me to process you. That's all I know. Please push your thumb on this ink pad and roll it on the paper," the cop replied when he finished typing. He also took her cell phone and placed it in a clear plastic bag.

The cop took her picture and made her sign some paperwork. When he was finished with her, he walked her over to a row of chairs and had her sit in the one farthest away from the gaggle of people in the middle of the room. Occasionally, she would hear Jack's loud and distinct laugh rise about the chatter.

Jack sounds drunk, and no one else seems to be enjoying themselves.

Kate sought out Sinclair. He was sitting in a chair in the opposite corner of the room. The people in the middle of the room mostly blocked her view of him so she only caught glimpses when people shifted around. She could not see Jo-Ellen at all.

Was this Amanda and Kyle's doing? Or the government's plan all along?

An hour after, Kate was guided to her seat, the people in the middle of the room split up. Several walked toward Kate and others headed toward Sinclair.

When the crowd broke up, Kate realized Jo-Ellen was on Sinclair's side of the room but sitting several rows away. They could speak to each other but would have to shout.

The acting general and other leadership at Space Force, the mayor, and several other high-ranking police officers sat down in chairs around Kate.

"Hello, Kate, how are you doing?" the acting general asked.

"Terrible. I'm thinking we are all going to have COVID as very few people are wearing masks. I thought D.C. was mask mandatory?" Kate asked, directing her question to the mayor. "Isn't that correct, Mayor?"

"We are in a huge warehouse. It's almost like being outside. And you are safe in your mask, so don't worry about what others are doing. Oh, and if what we are hearing is true, our lives are in far more danger from other sources than from COVID. Isn't that correct, Kate?" the mayor asked angrily.

THIRTEEN

Sixty-One Days After the Shooting

"We thought that 100-million-dollar piece of equipment Jack bought from you cleared the debris and should have cleared us with Rex, right? That is what you kept saying. We had to get rid of the dangerous space debris. We did it. Mission accomplished. But now the mayor's office has been told that you, Ms. Stellute, the woman that knows who or what caused the mass shooting, said more trouble is coming. What exactly is coming, Kate?" the acting general of Space Force asked.

Either Kyle and Amanda had betrayed her or their house was bugged. "First of all, *we* did it? I don't think so. That was all Sinclair, Jo-Ellen, Otter, Jack, and me. All you did was get in the way," she snapped, resisting the urge to remind him that Space Force also did a lot of threatening, following, lying, and dismissing of her and the truth. Not to mention the racist cops that tried to arrest Sinclair!

"And I don't have to say a word. I want a lawyer. I have rights. And, just to be clear, Jack did not buy the equipment from us. That money went from one billionaire to another. In fact, to that billionaire right over there," Kate said, nodding her head toward a man standing near Sinclair. "He got that money. Jack got the equipment. Sinclair and I just saved the world."

"Okay, young lady, I don't understand what happened in Florida or in space and I don't really care. But if we are going to have another mass shooting in my city, I need to know everything so that we can stop it," the mayor snapped.

"I want a lawyer," Kate repeated.

"Look, Ms. Stellute, this is a posh arrest location compared to where I can have you taken. The chief here is very eager to take you to real jail. You can wait there for a lawyer. No problem," the mayor said, crossing her arms in front of her chest.

"We were all celebrating in Florida. We thought we dodged bullets. Whatever you and Sinclair did seemed like a technological miracle. Then what happened? You spoke to Rex again and he was not happy?" the acting general of Space Force asked. "We are confused, Kate. We need you to clear this up."

The mayor sighed dramatically. "The report we got from one of our officers is that we are still in crisis and there will be more violence. We have to prevent it!"

Yes. I am well aware of that! I have to prevent it. I don't have time to wait for a lawyer and the slow crawl of justice. Working with the police has not ended well for me.

Kate jumped up, startling everyone near her. "Listen and listen very carefully," she shouted.

All eyes in the large room turned toward Kate. She had caught their attention, even if they could not hear her words. She spotted a pile of mylar blankets, protest signs, and cases of water in a corner of the room near her. On top of the water, she saw several bullhorns, probably confiscated from the protesters they processed in this building.

Kate walked quickly over to the corner and picked up a bullhorn and tried it out before any of the cops thought to stop her. It was a bit of a struggle with the handcuffs, but manageable. She fiddled with the buttons, remembering the one Kyle gave her as a Christmas present a couple of years ago.

"Testing, testing," Kate said into it, so loudly that people jumped and feedback crackled through the speaker.

"I have something I want to say to everyone." She cleared her throat. "I, uh, spoke to Rex the day before yesterday in the white room. If you didn't know, Rex is an extraterrestrial, or an avatar of one. Anyway, Rex was pleased with the removal of the pollution. He realized that by working together, we had made space safer for everyone and he reported that to the others. But he said the others were still coming. They may not have accepted that the work, our space garbage—oh excuse me, *debris*—removal was successful. Rex said they would not spend time understanding what we did and that they may cause more violence. He said they were coming soon." Kate paused, looking around the room at all the faces. No one said a word.

Some looked shocked, some angry, others incredulous, while Jack nodded his head, acting like he knew all along.

"I don't understand what all of that means either so there is no point in asking me any questions. That's all Rex said," Kate finished, lowering the bullhorn.

The room exploded with people shouting questions from all directions.

Kate ignored them and quickly walked over to Sinclair. "Are you okay?"

Sinclair stood as Kate approached him. She wanted to hug him, but they were both still handcuffed. "Yep. Fine. These Space Force people and Jack keep asking questions, but I refused to answer. This is your show, Kate. I'm just a helper." Sinclair nodded his head toward his interrogators.

"Sinclair has not said a single helpful or interesting thing!" Jack loudly exclaimed, sitting down in a chair near Sinclair.

Kate shook her head in disbelief. *He's so arrogant,* Kate thought. As if she would need Jack's confirmation that Sinclair was telling the truth!

"Shush. We're not supposed to be helping anyone, just listening," a man in a military uniform said to Jack.

Kate recognized him from the Space Force conference room but could not recall his name. She nodded at Malcolm who sat next to the man in uniform, but he did not nod back. She noticed he had a puffy lip and some bruises on his face.

"Though, I think you said enough," Sinclair whispered, leaning close so that only Kate would hear. His voice sent a shiver down her spine.

"What was that?" Malcolm asked, jumping up. He grabbed Kate's arm and the bullhorn and led her back across the room to where she had been sitting. "I thought they were not to speak to each other under any circumstances. But Jones whispered something to her. I did not hear what," Malcolm announced to the group as he pushed Kate back into her seat.

"Geez, Malcolm, what's your problem? Have a rough night?" Kate asked sarcastically, angry from being manhandled.

Malcolm looked at her with both anger and fear in his eyes.

"Why did you let that happen?" the acting general of Space Force angrily asked. He and the mayor had jumped up when Kate stomped over to pick up the bullhorn. They had been whispering to each other until Malcolm pushed Kate into the chair.

"I was so stunned you let her speak to the room, with a bullhorn, and then just let her walk over to Jones, that I briefly forgot to keep them separated," Malcolm snapped while waving the bullhorn around.

"What did Sinclair say, Kate?" the acting general asked.

"Sinclair said I have said enough," Kate replied honestly.

Throughout this whole ordeal, I just tell the truth and repeat myself again and again. No one listens. This is so frustrating and infuriating!

"No, you have not," the mayor said, sounding angry. "You need to tell us what Rex wants and how to prevent the violence. He must want something."

If I knew that, I would be out there executing a plan. Does no one understand what happened in Florida? What's wrong with these people?

"Nope. He did not say he wanted anything this time," Kate said.

"He just gave you a cryptic warning? Nothing else?" The mayor sat down across from Kate.

The officials who had guarded Sinclair and Jo-Ellen drifted closer during the altercation, blocking any view she had of Sinclair.

"Not really," Kate said. She did not lie, just left a part out. She hoped no one noticed.

"Not really? *Not really?* Tell us every fucking word he said!" the acting head of Space Force demanded, sitting down and putting his face close to Kate's.

Kate just sat in silence. This general needed to back up, give her space, and calm down before she said another word.

I did not tell Kyle the other part, so no one here knows about the Ark.

The acting general of Space Force and mayor pulled their chairs even closer to Kate in an intimidating manner. Kate just sighed. Thanks to Theo Mast and Rex, government officials and politicians didn't scare her at all anymore. Except that they could give her COVID.

Covid. It wasn't over, even though some liked to pretend the curve was flattened. "You need to back away now! Six feet away! I don't want to get COVID!" Kate snapped.

"Okay, okay," the mayor said, pushing her chair back. "Take her to jail. See if a night in the real-world slammer changes her mind."

"You *are* threatening *me*? The powers that be are threatening me? AGAIN!" Kate snarled, glowering at the acting general of Space Force. "Are you in agreement with the mayor about sending me to jail? Even though I have not broken a single law!"

"You can rot in jail for all I care," he replied, leaning back and crossing his arms.

"Oh my God! I've done nothing but tell you the truth since our first meeting. I warned you all about what Rex said he would do. I helped find a solution to clean up your bullshit pollution. All you have done is threaten and hound me. I can't believe we are still doing this!" Kate shouted. "And I will tell you something else. Rex told me he might bring me, and the people I love, up with him, and get us out of the way of the violence. So, I can just leave your selfish, polluting, threatening asses here to suffer the consequences of your choices and behavior." Kate pointed at the acting general of Space Force. "I know *exactly* what I will be thinking about when I'm in jail: when will I get off this planet and away from all of you assholes!"

"Take her away," the mayor instructed the chief of police.

As Kate was led out of the warehouse by two cops, her eyes sought out and found Sinclair's. His brows were furrowed. He pulled down his mask and mouthed the words "What happened?" Without the bullhorn to magnify her words, he could not hear what she had said.

Kate just shrugged. She knew he would be annoyed that she told them about the Ark.

FOURTEEN

Sixty-One Days After the Shooting

An hour later, Kate sat on the floor in a concrete cell in a D.C. jail with four other women. They were sitting on the benches and there was no space for Kate. One woman looked like a party girl or a prostitute, as her clothes were tight and revealing. One seemed to be having a mental crisis; she was breathing hard and could not stop crying. One looked like an angry teenager; Kate wondered if she was over eighteen. She was wearing a t-shirt with a cartoon character Kate did not recognize and jeans that were ripped in the right places to make them cool. The other was in a nice, but slightly disheveled, pinstriped suit. Everyone was wearing blue paper disposable face masks.

Kate sighed loudly, closed her eyes, and put her head in her hands.

The world could be coming to an end while I'm locked up, unable to do anything. Once again, the truth did not save me and it sure as hell did not set me free because I'm literally in jail.

Sitting in silence, Kate assigned the women nicknames to pass the time. The crier, Party Girl, the teenager, and Pinstripes all minded their own business until the one that seemed to be having a mental breakdown broke the silence.

"Are you the person that talks to space aliens?" the crier quietly inquired. Before Kate could answer, she wiped away her tears and stared directly at Kate. "Yep. You're that woman, Kate Stellute. My uncle says you talk to aliens. Is that true?"

Everyone looked at Kate.

She could shake her off and say she and her uncle were mistaken, maybe even accuse them of being crazy.

But it would be a lie.

"Yes, I'm Kate Stellute, and I've spoken to one extraterrestrial. He needed help cleaning up a dangerous mess in space that humans created."

"Wow, that's really cool," the crier sniffled, with tears pouring out of her eyes.

"Are you okay?" Kate asked her.

The woman just nodded and wiped away more tears.

"Yeah, I saw it online. I saw your picture. I thought the story was fake," the teenager said, sounding suspicious. Her legs were sprawled out, ensuring there was no extra space on her bench.

"I saw it on CNN and thought it was just another crazy story—people clinging to a reason for the mass shooting. Sure, space aliens, why not? Are you saying it's true?" the party girl asked.

"I'm not sure what you saw online or on the news, so I have no idea if what they reported is true. All I know is that I spoke to an extraterrestrial, or an avatar of sorts, a few times. It said it caused the mass shooting because of the dangerous debris and pollution we have put in space. I call him Rex," Kate explained.

"Yes. Rex. I heard that was his name!" the party girl said while nodding her head enthusiastically.

Huh, so the press knew his name now? They are actually calling him Rex?

Kate wondered how they learned that detail until it dawned on her: Kyle and Amanda. She hoped she was wrong. She didn't need or want another reason to be angry with Kyle. But she felt confident Space Force and NASA would not want that detail in the media.

"You helped ET clean up a mess? He killed millions of people and you helped it?" the teenager asked, her voice rising with each word. She sprawled out her legs even wider, letting Kate know there was definitely no space for her.

"Our pollution killed someone in space that was very special to Rex and his people. Rex caused the mass shooting as punishment. He demanded we clean up the mess to prevent more death here on Earth. If we didn't, he threatened to cause more violence, okay? I was terrified to even think what could be worse than a worldwide mass shooting. We thought, *hoped*, everything would be okay now. But it's not. There seems to be a problem," Kate said. She leaned her head back against the cold concrete wall and closed her eyes.

I can't believe I'm stuck in here when I should be out there, doing something! And I hope Sinclair is okay.

"So why are you in jail?" Pinstripes asked.

Kate opened her eyes and wrapped her arms around her knees.

"I don't know. I told the mayor, police, Space Force, and all the others exactly what I told you. They know it's true. I told the truth but the mayor had me brought here anyway. I guess they don't believe me," Kate replied.

"That's how life is. If people don't have the same experience as you, they won't believe you. And it'd better be the exact experience or they'll rip you apart and call you a liar. It's so unfair," the crier said between small sobs. "And, sometimes, they just don't want to believe you because they don't want to change or have to help you."

Kate nodded in agreement.

"Ain't that the truth," the party girl said. "But if you didn't break a law and they have not accused you of breaking a law, they can't hold you here. Have you made a call?"

"Nope. They brought me straight in here," Kate replied.

Who would I call? Sinclair and Jo-Ellen must be locked up too or they would be trying to get me out. Maybe they are? And Kyle, well, I can't trust him.

Kate assumed her mom couldn't help since she was in Florida—plus, it would upset her to no end. She doubted her colleagues or boss would take her call. Since Space Force made her a person of interest, no way they would get involved on her behalf against their employers. Most of Kate's close friends had left the area during the pandemic, fleeing the confines of city life for their hometowns and inexpensive rural places.

She felt helpless and frustrated, trapped in a cell when the world could be ending.

"I'm a lawyer. I have my own firm," Pinstripes said. "When they come for you, call my office and ask for Jim King. He'll come and get you or a member of his staff will. D.C. police might have broken the law in detaining you with no cause. We might be able to sue the city. You're very high profile. It'll get a lot of attention."

"Thanks. That's very helpful. I can't think of a single lawyer right now, at least, not any who practice criminal law," Kate said.

"Sure. Being in jail can be upsetting under normal circumstances and your situation is not normal. How did Rex cause the mass shooting?"

"I really don't know. He said he reads energy. I think he can also control it. I think that's how he made millions of people pick up their own guns and shoot themselves. It's pretty incredible to have that kind of power. Did you guys lose people in the shooting?" Kate asked.

All four heads nodded yes but no one spoke.

"I was lucky," Kate said, thinking of Theo Mast. "I didn't lose anyone close. Some people I know, of course, but no one I really loved. It's strange since more than 70 million Americans died. Almost seems statistically impossible. Of course, a few were close calls, meaning they were not near their guns during the fifteen-minute window."

"It's interesting how less violent the world has become. Sure, fewer people—which is very sad—means less violence, but fewer guns, well that has been wonderful. No one in my neighborhood has been shot since July. No gangbanger collateral damage or school shootings. No robberies gone wrong. I feel bad for so many of the souls that were lost in the shooting, but I also feel safer now. I mean, people can still be knifed of course, but you have to get really close for that. I'm just saying, no more cowards shooting from cars has been really nice. No one shooting into crowds or homes has been great," the party girl said. "Now, if the virus would just disappear, things, eventually, could be good again."

"I lost my brother and some close friends. Not ready to see a silver lining yet," the crier said as she wiped her eyes with her shirt.

"I'm a defense lawyer. I lost many friends and many clients. It may really cut into my business," Pinstripes said with a harsh laugh.

"Do you mind if I ask why you are in here?" Kate asked Pinstripes.

She asked me first so fair is fair.

"I'm a defense attorney with a drug habit. I got a little sloppy. It happens," Pinstripes replied with a shrug. "I blame the shooting and the pandemic."

"Are you worried you'll lose your license? Is it a felony charge? I'm not sure how it works but maybe that should be a concern?"

"Oh, I lost my license *years* ago. I am just an advisor at my firm now. I know the law inside and out and get people off all the time. I'm damn good at my job. The criminal justice system is corrupt. With the right amount of money, you can beat a rap almost every time. I will be out soon and on my merry way," she said. "I do like helping people, so I stay in the game."

"Can you help me? I would like to beat this charge and go on my merry way," the teenager said, sitting up from her deep slouch and leaning forward.

"What have they accused you of doing?" Pinstripes asked.

"Stealing a car," the teenager replied.

"Did anyone get hurt?" Pinstripes asked.

"Nope. But the Mercedes-Benz is a little beat up. It was just sitting there all shiny and beautiful, purring, with the keys in it. I just hopped in and drove around. It was so cool until the cops showed up and made me nervous," the teenager replied. "I don't know why I did it. It was really stupid now that I think about it."

Pinstripes laughed like it was the most hilarious story.

Maybe she's still high. She seems too happy.

"I'm feeling generous today and I have not been in jail for some time. And I'm here with some very lovely, interesting, and entertaining women. Just blame your troubles on the stress of the shooting and pandemic. We're all losing our minds! You can all call Jim King. Hell, he can help all of you," Pinstripes said, spreading her arms out wide. "Sometimes when they see his name, they drop the charges. Not worth all the trouble my firm can cause."

"Thank you!" the three women enthusiastically said at the same time.

The crier started to moan as big fat tears rolled down her cheeks and into her soaking-wet mask, which she pulled down briefly to wipe her nose on her sleeve. She was wearing shorts, a large, oversized t-shirt, and little blue paper socks rather than shoes, like patients wear in hospital wards.

"Are you sure you're okay?" Kate asked her again.

"Just having a bad day," she replied. "What kind of violence is coming next? You said Rex was bringing more violence. Who will he kill next?"

"It's not Rex but his, I guess, colleagues or super-visors that may commit more violence or revenge. He calls them 'the others.' And I have no idea what they will do. I assume it will not be guns again, but there are many other weapons that can be controlled and turned on their makers and users." Kate stood up to stretch and walk around.

Hopefully, Rex and his people will stay far away from nuclear bombs, which would hurt nature and wildlife—they did not cause this horrible situation.

"And there is no way to stop it?" the party girl asked.

"None that I know of. I don't think Rex knew of a way either," Kate said. "I think he would have told me if he did."

"I have a kid. A little girl. Her daddy died in the mass shooting," the party girl said, pulling her short skirt down. It had slid up so high that Kate could see her underwear.

"I'm so, so sorry for your loss," Kate said, swallowing the lump that formed in her throat. "For everyone's loss."

The teenager slid down the bench and indicated that Kate should sit next to her. Kate found the bench warmer and more comfortable than the floor, but not by much.

All the women sat in silence for a few minutes.

"I do have a question for all of you, if you don't mind. If you were given the choice to stay here, on Earth, and maybe die in the next round of vengeful violence, or go into space to live on a ship or another planet you have never seen or know anything about, what would you choose?"

"Is that an option or just a hypothetical?" Pinstripes asked.

"Not sure. No commitment. Just curious what you all would choose," Kate replied.

"I would go to space," the teenager said. "Get out of here. Explore something new. Die here or die there—what's the difference? Maybe space would be cool. Well, if I could take my boyfriend. He jumped in that car with me. Got in trouble with me. I would want him to come with me."

"I would go if I could take my daughter and mother with me. Maybe my sister, if she wasn't being a bitch. I would not mind getting out of here and being alive. Living sounds good," the party girl said.

"What if the aliens are mean? What if it's a trick and they want to kill us? What do they eat up in space? Bet they don't have pizza or tacos or ice cream. Can I take my dog? I think I would stay here. But I don't want to die, of course," the crier managed between small sobs.

"I feel an anxiety attack coming on just hearing the choices. Makes me feel like calling my dealer. Well, my other dealer since Greg is in jail too," Pinstripes said, laughing for a long time.

Yep, she must be high. That's just not funny at all.

Kate looked around at the women, studying their faces. These women all had lives and stories. They were dealing with the aftermath of the mass shooting and the COVID pandemic. They were here, in jail, under enormous stress, and yet, they were just being kind to each other.

"Well, let me know what you want. I can add you to a list. I might call it the Ark. Let me know the names of those you want to be added to it. Email or text them to me when you are released and get your phones back. My email is easy to remember since my name is now famous. I have no idea if space is good or safe. I have no idea how many people Rex can take. I have no idea if he can take dogs. I have no idea when Rex's colleagues will cause more violence or what kind. I have no idea what they eat. Think about all that and let me know if you want on the Ark," Kate said.

"Is it a sex thing? Like people have to be matched up?" the party girl asked. Her skirt had ridden up again and Kate could see flashes of neon pink.

"No. No, definitely not. I don't think," Kate responded.

Maybe calling it the Ark is a bad idea. Sinclair was right again.

"If what you are saying is true, if you can make a list, be careful with that power. You don't want to take mean, cruel people with you. Just take nice, sweet, good people," the crier said.

"Seriously. That is a really good point. You don't even know us. We could be crazy," Pinstripes added, slightly inclining her chin toward the woman that had not stopped crying.

"How can you tell if anyone is good? I don't want the mayor there or any leadership at Space Force. They are assholes. They are liars. But if you asked their friends and family, they would probably say they are all good people. It's impossible to tell," Kate mused.

"Well, make them think about it. Make them make a statement, a promise, that they are good and will be good. That might help," the party girl said, pulling her skirt down again.

"Make them sign a contract," Pinstripes suggested.

"What do you mean?" Kate asked.

"Prepare a contract," Pinstripes continued between giggles. "List the pros and cons clearly. 'You might die here or there. Where would you prefer to be at the end?' Make people that want to get on the list and go up into space sign a statement. Something like 'I am not an asshole and will not behave like an asshole in space.' Assuming this will be soon, you need to get the contract done and available to be signed fast." She stopped talking and succumbed to a full-on laughing fit.

"I realize you think this is a joke, but it's actually a great idea. People get to make their own decision. I just realized *that* is what was bothering Sinclair so much—that I was making the choice for people. He's so smart. But this idea, this contract, will make it an individual decision, governed by free will. Give people the facts—well, what few facts we have—and clearly state what kind of people they have to promise to be in space. I love it!" Kate exclaimed. "I can't wait to tell Sinclair about it!"

"Is Sinclair your hot boyfriend? I have seen pictures of him online. Sexy!" the teenager said, lightly smacking Kate's knee in her enthusiasm.

"Is the man you saw Black or White?" Kate asked.

"Black dude, older than you. Very dope," she replied.

"That's Sinclair. He's not my boyfriend. He has become, I guess, my best friend since the shooting. He has helped me so much. He's brilliant and kind. I never could have destroyed the pollution without him. He even went up in space, or wherever the hite room is, and met Rex. I would have lost my mind without Sinclair. I'm worried about him and I hope he is being treated well. If he's in jail, I hope his cellmates are as kind and supportive as mine," Kate said.

"Sounds like he should be your boyfriend," the teenager remarked

"Who *is* your boyfriend? Where is the White guy?" the party girl asked, pulling her drooping spaghetti strap up onto her shoulder.

"His name is Kyle. Not sure if there have been pictures of him online. I assume so since we live together and the press have staked out our house. I'm a little angry with Kyle. He doesn't believe me and he told a cop everything even after I asked him not to. Though, I had been withholding information from him, so some of the mistrust was my own fault. But I did tell him everything when I got back from Florida and he told a very beautiful cop and she told her bosses and they told the mayor and now I'm in jail. So, yes, I'm a little angry with Kyle," Kate said.

"Sinclair is brilliant and kind. You could not have survived without Sinclair. You're worried about *Sexy Sinclair* and the White boy has pissed you off. I think Sinclair should be your boyfriend," the crier said.

A cop appeared out of nowhere, startling all five women.

"Let's go, Stellute. People need to talk to you," the cop said as he unlocked the door.

"Remember ladies, email me your list of names," Kate said, slowly spelling out her email address. "In case I don't come back, it has been a pleasure getting to know you and serving time with you. And thank you for the great idea."

"You won't come back if you call Jim King at 202-777-7777. Think you can remember that number, Kate?" Pinstripes asked, no longer laughing.

"You know, they say the big house changes you. This time, that's very true," the crier called out as Kate was led away.

To freedom? Or something worse than jail?

FIFTEEN

Sixty-One Days After the Shooting

T he cop gave her back her phone on the way out. She wasn't being taken to make a phone call. Instead, she was escorted out of the jail and toward a squad car parked on the street. The temperature was still very high even though the sun was starting to set. A wave of exhaustion washed over her; it had been a long and trying day. And she was very worried about Sinclair.

Is he locked up too, being treated worse because of his color? While most of America's cops died in the shooting, it doesn't mean the young, new cops are necessarily any less racist.

"I'm not getting in a car until I see Sinclair Jones. Is he in jail?" Kate asked the cop guiding her toward the car.

"Who? That guy?" The cop gestured across the street and halfway down the block.

Kate's eyes locked with Sinclair's. Her heart exploded with relief.

And maybe something else.

He looked good. Safe. Unharmed.

And sexy.

Butterflies unleashed in her stomach as she trotted toward him.

Suddenly, the ground shook beneath her feet. The temperature plummeted.

Kate was flying.

She landed with a familiar thump in Rex's mysterious white room. She heaved over and over—her usual reaction to this weird form of transportation—but nothing came out. No surprise. She hadn't eaten all day and was dehydrated from her time in the slammer.

"Rex. Thank God!" Kate squawked out of her chattering teeth. She did not want to wait to warm up. Time was crucial. "W-w-w-we n-n-n-eed t-t-t-to t-t-t-talk!"

She pulled her knees close and rubbed her legs hard in an effort to warm up faster. Why did the white room, or space, or wherever Rex brought her, have to be so darn cold? She rocked back and forth.

"Okay. Better. Warmer," Kate said as soon as she could, looking at Rex across the room. "Have you heard from the others? Do you know their plans? Timing?" Kate asked as soon as her numb tongue and mouth could form a full sentence.

"Wait. Where's Sinclair?" Kate asked as she stood. She assumed Rex had pulled him up as well, but he was not in the white room.

She waited to let Rex respond. But after a moment, he still had not said a word.

"I do have an idea about the list if we still need it," Kate said, hoping he would say something.

The floor started to shake.

"No, Rex! What are you doing?" Kate screamed. "We need to talk!"

In her panic, her mind searched for something to engage him so he would not send her back.

"Why me?" Kate asked loudly, almost shouting.

The shaking abruptly stopped.

Thank God! Get him talking. I need information and answers.

"There was no logical reason for the collision. Just selfish, wasteful behavior. Humans have no respect for themselves or anyone else. I was going to destroy the planet and move on."

Jesus, he sounds so callous, so unlike the Rex I've come to know. Maybe Sinclair was right and the list wasn't such a good idea.

He flicked his thick, orange-striped tail. "While I was trying to understand why it happened, I watched your planet. The forests, oceans, and grasslands are teeming with unique and precious life. The trees and skies and mountains are so beautiful, the colors so vibrant. Between the color, the sound, the scents, and the constant motion, the energy on your planet is explosive. But humans don't see its beauty or care for it. They abuse nature in their own backyards just like they do in space. I decided: humans must die," Rex continued, in his slow cadence.

Kate didn't react. She was absorbed in his descriptions and explanation.

"Some humans love nature and wildlife. There are some good people. I saw them. They take care not to pollute or kill other beings. They try to treat the planet, nature, and people with respect and kindness. But these people aren't seeing what's happening in space. And those who use space as their dumping ground are a mystery to me," Rex said.

It was no mystery to Kate; the agencies, and people who ran them, didn't see beyond their own personal advancement and interest. They didn't get or care about the interconnectedness of all beings. Tears started to form in her eyes.

"I decided to learn more about those who pollute space. I studied the governments all over the world—and the people who work there. They all have one thing in common: they are *selfish*. Most of them do not even give pollution a single thought—not a single reflection on the harm this debris causes. NASA and Space Force dominate space and launch the most and are influential and they did nothing about the dangerous debris. As I watched and learned, I noticed *you*, Kate. A complicated human that loves nature and people and wildlife but works for an agency that callously pollutes. It was confusing." Rex continued, "You and your behavior intrigued me. Maybe all humans aren't bad. Maybe they don't all need to die."

Kate sat back down on the floor, afraid if she said a word, he would stop talking.

"I watched the people you admire," Rex said as his shape changed from Jane Goodall to Greta Thunberg to Jane Fonda to Neil Armstrong to Winona LaDuke to MaVynee Betsch to Katherine Johnson to John Lewis and Rachel Carson.

Kate gasped as she watched Rex's transformative slideshow.

"I watched you help people," Rex said as he became the manager at the homeless shelter and fellow volunteer at the animal rescue organization. "You know good people," Rex said becoming her mother and a friend who ran a lion conservation organization in Tanzania. "You care and you try to make things better, even when no one listens," Rex said as he became Leonardo DiCaprio, Al Gore, EO Wilson, and a local environmentalist Kate adored.

Kate nodded.

"I asked myself, what would Kate do? What does Kate hate most?" With that, he turned into a coronavirus.

"Who would Kate punish?" Rex asked, turning into Theo Mast.

Kate gasped and covered her face with her hands.

"The planet showed me that there is beautiful energy and life that must not be blamed for the pollution." Rex became an elephant, a polar bear, a sequoia tree, then a wolf. "You showed me there are good humans and bad," he said, becoming Theo Mast again, this time holding a big scary gun.

"For all your beautiful and kind energy, most humans have dark, cruel, and angry energy that comes from a place of fear. For those people, guns are the common denominator. When I made this connection, the solution was so simple. It only took a few minutes."

Kate stood up. Her hands were shaking and she felt a wave of nausea.

Did I do this?

"Did I choose the punishment?" Kate asked, her voice barely a whisper.

"You helped me choose the punishment, but you also helped me choose who and what to spare. You helped clean up space and made it safe. You are brave. I wish it had been enough. They are very close now. You must..."

Suddenly, the room shook.

"No! I have more questions!" Kate shouted just before she landed on her favorite trail in Rock Creek Park, a little over a mile away from her house.

SIXTEEN

Sixty-One Days After the Shooting

*W*hat the hell? *We were having an important discussion! Why did he send me back?*

Something is very, very wrong.

Kate jumped up from the awkward kneeling position she landed in on the trail.

"I need to talk to you! Bring me back! What's going on? I'm confused! I'm scared! Please, Rex, please pull me back up! We need to talk! I have an idea!" Kate shouted skyward.

She burst into tears of frustration and stomped down the trail to the road that led home.

"Kate!" Sinclair shouted as she emerged from the dark, wooded trail. "Oh, thank God! I had no idea how long you would be gone," Sinclair said, pulling her in for a tight hug. "I watched you disappear and knew Rex must have taken you up again."

She wiped her tears on his shirt.

"Are you okay?" he asked.

"No," Kate admitted, burrowing into his chest.

"What did he say? Are the others still coming? How much time do we have?" Sinclair asked, his warm breath ruffling the hair on the top of her head.

"How did you know to come here?" Kate asked.

"It was the only place I could think of since he grabbed you from around here twice before. Here or your backyard and this seemed more likely," Sinclair said.

Kate reluctantly pulled out of his arms. "How did you get here so fast?"

"Jo-Ellen was in her car on the street waiting for us. She was released from the warehouse and did not go to jail like we did. I told her I was pretty sure Rex had grabbed you. I asked her to take me to the trailhead where Rex harassed you," Sinclair said. "I was prepared to sit here all night. Jo-Ellen went to get food."

They slowly walked toward their street.

"What happened? Something bad, right?" Sinclair asked.

Kate took a deep breath. "It's really bad."

Sinclair reached for her hand, little prickles shooting up her fingers when they touched. "How bad?"

"He told me a story," Kate said, recounting Rex's long monologue about the beauty of the earth and how bad most humans were. She left out the part about her experience with Theo Mast being the inspiration behind the mass shooting. She knew she would start to bawl if she mentioned him and she did not have time for a crying fit. "But he seemed to get cut-off mid-sentence and sent me back."

"He can be awkward like that, right? Not completely unusual behavior," Sinclair reminded her, squeezing her still cold hand.

"No, this was different." Kate's mind raced. "Something is very wrong. We need to keep talking to him. I need to go back! He got cut off. There's more—I'm afraid we're in imminent danger," Kate said, breathing heavily.

Sinclair pulled her in for another hug and whispered, "It's going to be okay, Kate."

Kate took several deep breaths.

"I have no idea what is going on, Kate, but we will figure something out. Together. We're not giving up. Okay?" Sinclair pressed his forehead to hers.

Kate nodded a little. "Well, I did come up with a plan while in jail. I wish I could have discussed it with Rex," Kate said.

As they started to walk again, Kate thought of her plan and how she hoped Sinclair would like it.

At least we will be taking action, and it addresses his concerns because it provides for individual choice, so hopefully there will be no more arguing.

"Great. Lay it on me. Sitting alone in a cell for two hours provides a lot of time to think. I have some ideas as well," Sinclair said.

"I wasn't alone in jail. There were four other women in my cell. They were awesome. We talked and they helped me refine the idea. They gave me some really good suggestions."

Sinclair stopped dead.

"You didn't talk about Rex, did you? Say who you were? Tell them what happened? What we did?"

Sinclair asked, his voice sounding angrier and more afraid with each question.

Damn, he is upset again. So much for getting back to normal.

"Well, yes. They recognized me. They knew things already. So yeah, we talked. I mean, what else does one do in the big house but bond with fellow prisoners, right?" Kate joked, trying to lighten the mood.

"Kate, they have cameras in jail cells. I have no idea if the police can record conversations, but I am damn sure Space Force could have it done under these extreme circumstances. I bet they have your entire conversation recorded!" Sinclair groaned "What exactly did you say?"

"I don't know. We talked about everything, I think. And a lawyer gave me advice for how to ensure the plan works for everyone," Kate wailed, upset with herself for not considering cameras. She started walking fast toward home.

Home. Is it my home or Kyle's? Will he be there? Maybe Amanda is there too. When did everything get so messed up?

Sinclair jogged to catch up with her fast pace. "Kate. It will be okay. We'll figure something out. I'm sorry I snapped. That was uncalled for. Let's go to my place and see what Jo-Ellen found for dinner. With food, we will think more clearly. It's been a long, stressful day. We will sort this out together. Okay?"

Sinclair was good. He was kind. And he was, as her cellmates said, sexy. They may have said that on camera. Kate cringed at the thought. She'd made an idiotic mistake and here was Sinclair, trying to make her feel better. She tried to recall exactly who said

Sinclair was sexy and what she had said about Kyle and Amanda! Sinclair thought she was upset about revealing information about Rex but whatever—she really liked her cellmates and didn't care who knew the truth about Rex. But she felt a wave of nausea thinking about what she'd said about Sinclair and Kyle. She'd die of embarrassment if that conversation was publicly released.

SEVENTEEN

Sixty-One Days After the Shooting

Holding hands and sticking to the dark side of the pathway, Sinclair and Kate cut through Sinclair's alley, snuck through his extra-large back fence door, into his little backyard, and up the porch stairs to his house.

In case he was home—and worse, had his cop with him—she wanted to avoid alerting Kyle that they were back.

Likewise, Jo-Ellen snuck in through the back, bringing with her wine and dinner, which they ate in the dark on the back porch to maintain the illusion that no one was home. They devoured their dinner in silence.

"Thanks, Jo-Ellen. This is perfect, really hits the spot. I didn't realize how hungry I was," Kate whispered between bites. She was nervous that on the back deck, anyone could be listening in on their conversation like Jo-Ellen once had.

Kate finished eating and walked out into the backyard to look up at the moon.

Please, hear the new plan, Rex. Don't destroy all of humanity without at least considering my new approach to saving the lives of good and decent people.

Kate waited, wanting to feel Rex whip her away to the white room.

But Rex gave no response. She sighed and returned to the porch, sitting on a lower step and looking up at Sinclair and Jo-Ellen. "Why do you think they took us to the warehouse? Posh jail? And then regular jail? Why not Guantanamo Bay or a secret CIA torture chamber? I mean, they keep saying they don't believe me so why not pull out my fingernails or something to make me tell the truth?" Kate quietly asked.

"That's funny because I heard Malcolm was suggesting that at some point when we were in Florida. The suggestion was supposedly shot down because the people comfortable with torture—I mean, intense interrogation—are mostly dead," Jo-Ellen replied. "Oh, and that reminds me, something really strange happened to Malcolm today."

Kate's eyes grew large. "What happened?"

"Malcolm called me while you two were in jail. He told me a story and wanted me to tell it to you, Kate. And he wanted me to clearly tell you that it was not his idea. He repeated that many times, that none of it was his idea," Jo-Ellen replied. "I almost forgot in our panic to find you."

"Okay, so tell me. What was not Malcolm's idea?' Kate asked.

"Malcolm said **Acting General White** was contacted by an unnamed military or spy organization. Specifically, two agents that claimed they represented some organization or agency. Who knows if that is true? I mean, White is the head of Space Force, I would assume he is working closely with the Department of Defense, CIA, and FBI. But there is mass confusion in the government right now." Jo-Ellen sighed loudly. "Anyway, it seems they were advocating to use harder measures to make Kate give them Rex. White told Malcolm to meet them and find out what was going on. Malcolm said he met them at one of their apartments last night. Malcolm said it was him, the two spooks or whatever they are, and one of their girlfriends. They drank beer and talked about you, Rex, and the situation."

"I don't think they were real agents. That does not sound professional. I hope Malcolm did more listening than talking," Sinclair remarked.

Jo-Ellen shrugged. "It gets stranger. Malcolm said the direction of the conversation was violent and made him uncomfortable, but he agreed to meet with them in the morning because White asked him to check it out. As Malcolm got near the apartment this morning, he saw one of the supposed agents, also driving to the apartment. The guy was driving right in front of him and they got blocked at a light by another car. I don't remember all the details but there was horn honking and yelling and a fender bender. Malcolm was not involved in the accident; he just watched it. I remember him clearly saying that."

Joe-Ellen paused and Kate nodded her head encouraging her to continue.

"Malcolm said he got out of his car and rushed to the agent's car and when he looked in the window, the guy was gone. The car was empty. The car was still running, I guess idling against the other car's back bumper, but the car was empty. Malcolm said it was like he vaporized into thin air. It took Malcolm seconds to get out of his car and to the driver's window, but the guy was gone." Jo-Ellen paused dramatically to take a sip of wine.

"What the hell! Where did he go?" Kate asked.

"It gets even stranger," Jo-Ellen replied. "Malcolm said when he finally got to the apartment, the girl-friend from the night before was crying hysterically. She said her boyfriend, the other supposed agent, was in the shower for a long time, and when she finally went in to check, the shower was empty. The water was running and his clothes were there, everything, but no secret agent boyfriend. So, Malcolm told her what happened to the other dude, the fender bender disappearance, and she really flipped out."

"No kidding! That is crazy! What happened next?" A chill ran down Kate's spine.

"Malcolm said he told the girlfriend '*maybe Rex took them*' and she lost it. She yelled it was Malcolm's fault for encouraging them and she hit him so he left. He did look pretty banged up at the warehouse," Jo-Ellen mused.

"So where are the agents? Who did they work for? Who is investigating this now?" Sinclair demanded. "Kate could be in serious danger!"

"I don't know. I got a text saying they were releasing you so I hung up on Malcolm and went to look for you two. Then I got all caught up in finding Kate after her latest Rex encounter. And now here we are." Jo-Ellen took another large sip of wine. "I will call Malcolm in the morning to make sure I got his story right and see if anything else happened."

"Rex watches you and he is extremely powerful. What would Rex do to someone that wanted to hurt you? I mean, he killed hundreds of millions of people. Who would take on the job of pissing Rex off? Maybe these guys were planning to hurt you? Until they put you in jail, Space Force and DOD and everyone just followed you, as Jo-Ellen said, hoping they could get to Rex when he communicated with you," Sinclair said, looking at Kate.

"Huh, like when interrogation was suggested. It appears that no one volunteered for that dangerous, and stupid, job," Jo-Ellen said.

Kate just slowly nodded, processing the strange story.

Did Rex take those men? Did he hurt those men? Is Rex protecting me?

Confused about how to feel, Kate started to breathe heavily, and tears formed in her eyes.

"So, what happened in real jail, anyway?" Jo-Ellen asked, changing the subject. She was watching Kate closely and saw the tears appear.

Kate appreciated the distraction and told her what had occurred in jail—leaving out the part about some of the ladies recommending she ditch Kyle for Sinclair. She said she met a disbarred attorney that recommended a lawyer at her firm that might sue D.C. for false arrest. Kate explained that she had chatted with her cellmates about Rex after they said they recognized her from the media. She explained that the ladies thought it was important that Rex only take good people, and how the lawyer provided a good suggestion to do so, and offered a lawyer at her firm to help with the contract.

"I need a computer. I want to draft the contract tonight and send it to the lawyer, Jim King, tomorrow. Hopefully, he'll help. Once it's passed legal muster..." Kate paused to wonder what constituted *legal* in outer space. "...I'll make it available to people so they can decide if they want to be taken up before the violence starts. People can make their own decision." Kate smiled at Sinclair, waiting for his assurance that this plan was better.

"Kate, I really think—" Sinclair began.

"—I think this plan addresses your fundamental concern that I was making a huge decision for people," Kate interrupted. "You were right, Sinclair; I should not have that power. This way they can decide for themselves. But I'm worried we're running out of time. Why did Rex grab me and send me back so abruptly? We need this done immediately. I'm sorry if you are still upset about the Ark—I mean, the list— but we just don't have time to debate it further. The others could kill us all at any moment! I'm so angry with Rex. And Kyle too," Kate grew more upset and frantic with each word she spoke.

Time could be running out! To that end, why are we just sitting out here eating and drinking wine like the world couldn't just end at any moment?

"Kate, I'm not talking you out of your plan. It has been a very long day. I think we all need some sleep. How about your write the Ark contract in the morning?" Sinclair asked.

"We don't have time to wait, Sinclair. And I've decided not to call it the Ark anymore. It confuses people. They seem to think it's a matchmaking thing. You were right about that too," Kate snapped, irrationally annoyed that he was right again.

"And we need to go over what you said in the jail cell, in case we need to be prepared for any fallout tomorrow, but I agree with Sinclair: sleep first. You could tell me everything now and I fear I would just nod my head like I'm listening and forget it all. We can discuss everything in the morning," Jo-Ellen said.

We will discuss the details about what was said about Rex and the Ark—I mean, the list—but not Sinclair and Kyle.

Kate hoped they couldn't see her blush.

"You'd better hope they didn't capture your jailbird conversation on camera. I doubt it would be helpful to have end-of-the-world choices leaked to the press before you flesh it out," Sinclair said, igniting more worry in Kate's stomach.

"That's why we need to act quickly. According to my cellmates, a lot about me and Rex is out in the public already. The cat, or rather, *Rex*, is out of the bag. Why did Rex bring me up to just send me back so quickly? I had important questions. It's so frustrating!" Kate said, jumping around between subjects and finding it difficult to keep her eyes open. The food and wine made her loopy and she slouched on the porch stairs. "I may have really screwed everything up. I'm sorry," she mumbled.

"Well, I don't know how you two are still awake given the day you've had. I'd better get going before I fall asleep on Sinclair's porch and get eaten alive by mosquitoes. Good night, Kate," Jo-Ellen said as she walked down the steps and through the gate to her car parked in the alley.

Sinclair took Kate's hands and pulled her to her feet, their chests inches apart. She could sense the beating of his heart, feel the warmth exuding out of him.

Her stomach did a flip.

"Come on, time for bed," he said.

Bed? Where will I sleep?

With an arm firmly wrapped around her waist, he guided her through the dark house and upstairs. Steering her into a bedroom, his bedroom, he gently pushed her back onto the mattress. The butterflies churned frantically in her stomach as she wondered if he would sleep here too.

But Sinclair did not recline next to her. Standing at the foot of the bed, he took off her shoes, one by one, the thump they made on the floor when he dropped them not nearly as loud as her beating heart.

He ran a thumb up the sole of her arch.

She closed her eyes and stifled a moan at how good the pressure of his touch felt.

But then he released her feet and pulled a blanket from the closet, draping it over her body. "Good night, Kate," he whispered as he tucked her into his bed. He planted a kiss on her forehead before backing out of the room and turning off the light.

EIGHTEEN

Sixty-Two Days After the Shooting

Kate jerked awake from a horrible dream. Shaking, she looked frantically around the room, not sure where she was. In her dream, everything in D.C. was on fire: homes, trees, monuments. People were running and screaming and burning alive. Dead, charred animals littered the streets like she had seen on the news during horrific wildfires caused by climate change.

With her heart still thumping, Kate jumped out of bed and quickly searched the room for clues.

This is Sinclair's room.

She could smell him and feel his presence. She took a few deep breaths to calm down and reminded herself she was alive and safe. There was still time.

Kate used the bathroom, freshened up, and went downstairs.

Sinclair had left a laptop open and a note that read "Kate—feel free to use this computer, the password is 77starwarslove."

Kate smiled as she logged in and started typing up the contract:

> Whereas, I understand that Rex, an extraterrestrial, caused the mass shooting on July 14, 2020, resulting in hundreds of millions of gun-owners turning their weapons on themselves.

> Whereas, I understand that Rex caused the mass shooting as punishment because the people of Earth polluted space with debris and garbage and made it unsafe for everyone in space.

> Whereas, Rex asked that the dangerous debris be removed from space or he would cause more violence.

> Whereas, everyone worked together, including several individuals working with NASA and Space Force, and pulverized all the space debris and made space safe on September 7, 2020.

> Whereas, on September 11, 2020, Rex informed the people of Earth, through a messenger, that others of his kind were coming and may cause more global violence, despite the clean-up.

> Whereas, I understand there MIGHT be an opportunity for Rex to take me into space and spare my life from the pending wrath and violence.

Whereas, I understand this document is about making a choice to stay on Earth and die or travel into space and live with Rex.

Whereas, I acknowledge and understand that I have no idea what living in space will be like. It may be very dangerous and scary or fantastic—I have no idea. I only know it will not be like Earth. I'm not sure what we will breathe.

Whereas, I chose to go into space with Rex to avoid violence on Earth.

In order to go into space with Rex, I certify, by signing this contract, that I will uphold these principles:

I will never use a weapon against my fellow humans or any extraterrestrial.

I will never leave garbage anywhere and will aggressively ensure any waste products caused by my actions, consumption, or work, either directly or in-directly, will be properly and safely disposed of, or I will not take such action, consumption, or work.

I will not eat animals as it causes water pollution, air pollution, habitat destruction, climate change, the biodiversity extinction crisis, and scares and hurts animals. I do not know if there will be animals, as humans understand them, in space, but I will not hurt them or their habitat if there are.

I will always treat my fellow humans and extra-terrestrials with kindness and respect, including with justice and equity, and I will support diversity and inclusiveness for all, regardless of their species, race, religion, sex, or sexual identity.

I will never lie or deceive anyone.

I will never steal or cheat anyone or anything out of their possessions, dignity, or needs for survival or happiness.

I will always reflect on all of my actions and learn about and take into consideration all impacts and consequences to others, including all species, wildlife, nature, and space.

Kate was so involved with her task at hand that she jumped when Sinclair came through the back door carrying groceries.

"Hey, Kate. Good morning. How did you sleep?" Sinclair asked as he put things away. "I'll make some coffee in a minute. I didn't realize how empty this kitchen was until I woke up and wanted coffee."

Kate's face flushed red remembering his gentle touch the night before.

"I slept fine, thank you. Except for some terri-fying nightmares. I would love some coffee, please. Thank you."

Do I sound oddly formal and nervous? I have to stop being so weird. It wasn't like we slept together. I mean, we have slept together before, but we didn't have sex or anything...

Jesus, Kate, pull yourself together!

As Sinclair prepared breakfast, Kate reread her work.

Sinclair was probably going to hate it. But she would not have made it to this point without him so she needed to convince him this was the right thing to do.

As they sat down to eat, Kate slid the laptop over to him. "Please read this and let me know what you think. It's a very rough draft," Kate said.

She tried not to watch his face for a reaction as he quickly read her contract.

"Well, seems like you have made every effort to ensure that the humans that choose to live with Rex will be on their best behavior. Of course, this will not have any impact on how Rex and the others treat the humans. And it has a couple of typos and poor grammar," Sinclair said, sounding cross again.

"I said it was a rough draft," Kate snapped back, reaching for the laptop.

They both jumped when the back door opened.

"Good morning! How is everyone feeling today? Ready to save the world again?" Jo-Ellen asked as she walked in.

Neither Sinclair nor Kate said a word.

"What happened?" Jo-Ellen asked, sensing the tension in the room. "Did you talk to Rex? Or did you two hook up?"

Kate blushed to her hairline. Sinclair cleared his throat. "Of course not," he managed. He seemed to choke on the words and cleared his throat again.

Do I detect regret in his voice? Nerves? Desire? Or is he just embarrassed by the question?

"Ah, too bad. Is it Rex then?" Jo-Ellen went through Sinclair's cabinets like she lived there and helped herself to a cup of coffee.

"No, not Rex," Sinclair said, regaining the normal timbre of his voice. "Kate is attempting to create nirvana for humans in space. It could be a perfect world. And you know how a huge change, stress, and fear bring out the best in people. I mean, just look at this pandemic."

"I just want people to know what they are getting into if they want the opportunity to leave Earth. I mean, if it's actually possible for Rex to take a lot of humans with him. I just want people to treat each other and their environment with real kindness—no matter where they are. I'm going to send this over to Jim King and see if he can make it into a contract," Kate said, passion rising in her voice.

We've lived through so much horror in such a short period of time. Why not try to create and live in nirvana?

Kate picked up the laptop and started to walk out of the kitchen but paused in the doorway. "Have some breakfast, Jo-Ellen. Fuel up. We've no idea what'll happen today."

Jo-Ellen flashed Sinclair a worried look. He shrugged.

Kate continued: "Or if we will even survive it."

NINETEEN

Sixty-Two Days After the Shooting

An hour later, Kate had all the affirmation she needed.

"Jim King thinks I am some kind of folk hero, and he was very helpful," she reported to Sinclair and Jo-Ellen. "He said what I drafted can't be made into a legal contract. There's no time to make it applicable to so many different people since it will be open to the public. Nor can he make it be legally binding in space." She laughed and again wondered what terms like *legal* and *contract* meant in Rex's world. "He's funny. And he doesn't think I'm completely nuts, so that's a plus."

Kate put the laptop down and refilled her coffee cup.

"Then why are you so happy?" Sinclair asked.

"Because he made it into a pledge. And he corrected the typos and grammar," Kate said.

"May I read it?" Jo-Ellen asked.

"Sure, feel free to make edits. The more eyes on it, the better." Kate handed the laptop to Jo-Ellen.

While Jo-Ellen read the document, Kate and Sinclair stared at each other. She mentally dared him to criticize her plan.

It wasn't like he had anything better to offer. Also, why do I feel so edgy looking into his eyes? Hopefully, he thinks this deep red blush is anger, not attraction. I need to pull myself together and focus on getting this done and out and stop thinking about Sinclair!

"Add something about democracy. I know all Earthlings won't agree, but most should prefer a one-human, one-vote type government if given an option. And maybe something about the arts? Investment and appreciation for the arts are often left out of important documents, but creativity is such an important part of being human. Oh, and science!" Jo-Ellen typed as she spoke. "I won't add anything about the justice system because, frankly, why would we need it with all the other provisions?" Jo-Ellen laughed. "This is fun!"

"Creating an even more perfect world, maybe just drop our Constitution in it, but change 'men' to 'Earthlings' and leave out the second amendment," Sinclair said, smiling in a relaxed manner.

"What are you going to do with it?" Jo-Ellen asked as she finished typing. "Do you think people will sign it?"

"I don't know. I'm just giving them the opportunity. They make the choice," Kate replied.

"Do people even sign petitions anymore? I feel like there are so many petitions. I get requests to sign petitions every day, sometimes several. Do I support a free press? If so, sign a petition! Do I support democracy? Abortion rights? Universal healthcare?

Banning animal experimentation and factory farms? Equal pay? Stopping the fossil fuel industry from cooking the planet? There's a petition for every issue, and they never seem to work. Are they even delivered? Do the powers that be even care? I mean, it takes like a second to click 'yes', so maybe they are just too easy to matter anymore. People click 'yes' and feel good and nothing changes," Jo-Ellen remarked.

"They generally do seem pointless. But maybe it's better than doing nothing?" Kate asked, without expecting an answer. "And this is a *pledge*, not a petition. A pledge is a personal declaration, a solemn promise, a real commitment."

"Remember when the Obama Administration got so many petitions, they wouldn't read them unless they had like 50,000 or maybe 500,000 signers, in like thirty days? I can't remember the details. Nothing really came from those efforts. Petitions became toothless. Anyway, if it is a matter of life or death, lots of people will probably sign it," Jo-Ellen said. "Or they'll think it's insane and will laugh it off. Could go either way."

"Jo-Ellen, it's a pledge, not a petition. It will arrive in email inboxes and be all over social media, I guess it'll look similar to a petition, but it's actually a pledge. Pledges carry more weight, more of a commitment. At least that is what Mr. King told me," Kate said, taking the laptop back from Jo-Ellen.

"But there are consequences to signing petitions and pledges. People have lost their jobs by signing petitions. Remember that cool environmentalist that was working in the Obama White House that got fired for signing a petition, years earlier, that said the previous administration should be investigated and impeached for lying to America about the reasons we invaded Iraq? Do you remember the yellow cake lies? That whole thing was outrageous because the environmentalist was right—that administration should have been impeached for lying to start a war. That guy, the environmentalist, should not have been fired: pledge or no pledge," Sinclair said with disgust.

"That is why we have the 'no lying' provision in the *pledge*," Kate said.

Sinclair sighed. "That wasn't really my point. The thing is, petitions, or pledges, that seem harmless at one time, can have serious consequences at another. Very serious consequences. And, with this one, if you sign it, Rex can pull you into space and who knows what will happen there! I think that is a more important consideration than it being legally binding," Sinclair snapped.

"I wish it could be legally binding. I hope everyone who signs it considers it so. I want them to think very, very seriously before they sign it," Kate snapped back at him.

"Well, at least we agree on that," Sinclair murmured.

"Do you think it's too preachy, Jo-Ellen? I don't want to be preachy," Kate said, scanning the document one more time.

Jo-Ellen and Sinclair burst into robust laughter.

"Ha, coming from anyone but you, it would definitely seem too preachy!" Jo-Ellen said. "But considering what you've seen and experienced and done, nope, not too preachy."

"Good. Thanks. Because I am going to hit send," Kate replied.

"Done," she announced three seconds later, while dramatically hitting a key.

TWENTY

Sixty-Two Days After the Shooting

"**W**ait, who did you send it to?" Sinclair asked, choking a bit on his coffee.

"Everyone I know—and the press and Space Force and the mayor's office," Kate said as she typed. "What can I hashtag? I need it to go viral on social media. Oh, never mind, I'll let others make that decision. Maybe some influencers will get involved. My name is out there and connected to Rex and the mass shooting. I'm counting on my infamy to get attention and help it spread."

Within minutes, the pledge with a signature link was being circulated around the country.

<u>I Choose to Live in Space, Rather Than Die on Earth Pledge – September 2020</u>

Whereas, I understand that Rex, an extraterrestrial, caused the mass shooting on July 14, 2020, which resulted in hundreds of millions of gun owners turning their weapons on themselves.

Whereas, I understand that Rex caused the mass shooting as punishment because the people of Earth polluted space with debris and garbage and made it unsafe for everyone.

Whereas, Rex asked that the dangerous debris be removed from space or there would be more violence.

Whereas, several individuals, working with NASA and Space Force, pulverized all the space debris on September 7, 2020, and made space much safer for everyone.

Whereas, on September 11, 2020, Rex informed the people of Earth that others of his kind were coming and may cause more global violence, despite the clean-up.

Whereas, I understand there MIGHT be an opportunity for Rex to take me into space and spare my life from the pending wrath and violence on Earth.

Whereas, I understand I have a choice to stay on Earth and die or travel into space.

Whereas, I acknowledge and understand that I have no idea, nor does any other human, what living in space will be like. It may be dangerous, scary or even deadly, or fantastic—I have no idea. I only know it will not be like Earth.

Whereas I choose to go into space with Rex to avoid violence on Earth and I make this decision of my own volition.

In order to go into space with Rex, I pledge to do the following:

I will never use a weapon against my fellow humans or any extraterrestrial;

I will never leave garbage anywhere and will aggressively ensure any waste products caused by my actions, consumption, or work, either directly or indirectly, will be properly and safely recycled or disposed of, or I will not take such action, consumption, or work;

If animals go into space or any are encountered in space, I will not eat them. Since the consumption of animals on Earth caused water pollution, air pollution, habitat destruction, climate change, disease and illness, the biodiversity extinction crisis, and scares and hurts them, out of an abundance of caution and concern all around, I will not eat any animals;

I will always treat my fellow humans and extraterrestrials with kindness and respect, including with justice and equity. I will support diversity and inclusiveness for all, regardless of their species, race, disability, color, religion, planet of origin, sex, or sexual identity;

I will respect and encourage creative and peaceful scientific research, education, and artistic expression;

I will never lie, steal, cheat, or deceive anyone or anything;

I will not be selfish;

I will always reflect on all of my actions and learn about and take into consideration all impacts and consequences to others, including all species, wildlife, and nature, whatever form they take in space;

I will always support a purely democratic government with one-human, one-vote, and will support free speech;

I take this pledge, not holding any human or extraterrestrial responsible, and assume all personal risk willingly and not under any duress.

Name:
Address:
Email:

If animals can be safe in space and pets are allowed, I would like to bring (pet name/species):

Kate, Sinclair, and Jo-Ellen stared at their screens, watching the pledge spread across social media.

"I'm just taking a minute to picture nirvana. It would be an amazing world. Too bad we didn't live like this before the mass shooting," Kate said with her eyes closed.

"So, now that that is finished, what is the plan moving forward? I hate to push, but I think getting to Rex is really important. We need more information," Jo-Ellen said, putting her phone down.

"We have no control over Rex. I'm very worried. His grabbing me and talking and then dropping me so fast, literally, mid-sentence, was weird. Something's very wrong. That's why we needed to get this pledge going," Kate said.

Sinclair was silent, watching her.

Is he still angry? He always hated the list/Ark/pledge idea. I want to hug him. Be a team again. Climb on his lap…

"So, what do we do now?" Jo-Ellen asked again.

"We wait," Kate blushed, looking away from Sinclair. "It's all we can do now."

TWENTY-ONE

Sixty-Two Days After the Shooting

They all jumped at the loud banging on the front door.

"Didn't have to wait long," Sinclair said as he headed toward the door.

"Kate!" Kyle called as he pushed past Sinclair. "Where are you?"

Shit. Am I ready to see him? Can I deal with this right now?

She didn't have but a few seconds to brace herself. "Right here, Kyle, in the kitchen," Kate called, resigned to the conversation that was about to occur.

"What is that pledge? Is that a fucking joke? We're going to die if we stay on Earth? Why didn't you say so yesterday?" Kyle asked in a rush as he entered the kitchen. He nodded at Jo-Ellen. "You sneak out of the house without saying goodbye, and Amanda informs me you were *arrested?* I hear no word from you, I'm worried sick, and then I get an email asking me to sign a strange pledge!"

"Want some coffee, Kyle?" Sinclair asked.

"Okay, sure, thanks Sinclair," Kyle said without looking at him.

Kyle gripped the sides of his head as if trying to contain his anger. "But that pledge? Come on, Kate! First, it's ridiculous. No one is going to commit to all that. I mean, sure, it would be awesome if they did, but they won't. Second, it's a lot to ask of people, I guess to be clear, *humans*. If *humans* stay home, *on Earth*, will the E.T. shoot them? Everyone?"

Kate took a deep breath and reminded herself that she had to stay calm, that she was doing the right thing. "I have no idea. Like I told you yesterday, Rex said there was a problem. His people, the others as he calls them, didn't accept the clean-up as payment for killing their VIPs. Do you believe me now? You and Amanda seemed pretty incredulous yesterday."

"Well, what you were saying was pretty unbelievable," Kyle replied, his face flushed with anger.

"Kyle, I didn't have time to waste trying to convince you that I was telling the truth. Why would I lie?" Kate asked, getting flushed herself. "And it's pretty sad when the person you're closest to doesn't believe you."

She watched him wince.

While she normally would never want to hurt Kyle, she felt like it was a small victory. She was very angry because he had somehow managed to betray her trust while not believing her.

"Whatever. I mean, I'm over it. Space Force, NASA, the mayor, cops, and some rich assholes didn't believe me either. And as you know, they put us in jail," Kate said.

"Amanda said they took you to the warehouse jail for processing. She said it doesn't have cells, it's clean, just for Capitol Hill protestors, not real criminals," Kyle said.

"We were, but they moved me and Sinclair to real jail." She looked at Sinclair, leaning against the counter, a cup of coffee cradled in his hands. "I spent a couple of hours in real jail with real people that had been accused of actual crimes. Though my cell-mates were pretty cool," Kate added.

"Seriously? Amanda didn't mention that," Kyle replied, looking from her to Sinclair and back to her before taking a long sip of coffee.

So, he believes Amanda again over me. He must have it bad for Amanda. I wonder if he even realizes it. He does not seem to be thinking clearly. And is he looking to Sinclair for confirmation that I'm telling the truth?

Jo-Ellen's, Sinclair's, and Kate's phones all started going off simultaneously. Texts and calls screamed for their attention.

"Sorry, Kyle. We all need to take these. We're really busy. I'll come over later and we can talk," Kate said, answering her phone.

"Hi, Kate Stellute? This is Julie from FOX News. May I ask you a few questions?" a reporter asked before Kate could say a word.

Kate stayed on the call, not saying anything until Kyle walked out. "Sorry, no, I am not talking to the press right now, but thanks for calling," Kate said in her most cheerful voice before hanging up.

"Space Force, NASA, reporters, calling all of us. How do you want to handle this, Kate?" Sinclair asked. "I'll do whatever you want."

Kate smiled at him. "I don't know. Any ideas?"

"How about we schedule a few specific interviews? Like CNN, local D.C. news, FOX, Washington Post, and a few others. That'll help get the pledge out more broadly. You can explain why you created it. It might help give it credibility. See what people decide to do," Sinclair suggested.

"I can do it. Give me an hour to set them up. I'll act as your communications director. What do you think?" Jo-Ellen asked.

Kate went over and hugged her. "Thanks, Jo-Ellen. That sounds fantastic. I'm happy you're here. I'm going to go home and take a shower and put on proper clothes and make-up so I look good for the interviews. I need to look trustworthy and you know, not disheveled and frazzled."

Jo-Ellen nodded as she pulled out of the hug and smoothly took another call. "The only person at CNN Kate will talk to is…"

Kate did not wait to hear who the only person she would speak to at CNN was. She walked out of the kitchen and toward the front door. Sinclair rushed to open it for her.

"You should bring your things here. More clothes, products, computers, whatever you need. Stay here as long as you want. Do you want me to come with you?" Sinclair asked.

"No, but thanks. I can talk to Kyle as I get ready," Kate said. "I'm sure he has many more questions."

Sinclair nodded his head and averted his eyes.

"But I'll call you when I'm done and ready to come back. I might need you to help me carry stuff," Kate added.

Sinclair smiled broadly and pulled Kate in for a hug.

He smells so good. I feel so safe right here with him. I want to stay in his embrace and absorb his constant good, supportive energy.

But we don't have time for this.

"I'll be back soon," Kate said, pulling away.

TWENTY-TWO

Sixty-Two Days After the Shooting

An hour later, Sinclair pulled Kate's suitcase and carried a large box across the street. Kate lugged her overstuffed backpack and a box with her favorite coffee mug, reusable water bottle, books she was currently reading, and a couple of pictures of her and her mom. She was grateful that Sinclair responded quickly to her text for help.

"I didn't know what to bring. It's so confusing," Kate said as they slowly walked. "I wasn't expecting to break up with my boyfriend in the middle of yet another global crisis." She tried to make it sound funny but her words fell flat.

"How did it go? Where is Kyle?" Sinclair asked.

"He went to Amanda's place. I tried to make him understand that none of this was my fault. I did not intentionally meet Rex. I don't have any control over anything. But he seems to think I do, like I should have just walked away from the situation. He's still struggling with believing me. I mean, it is unbelievable. I get it. And he reminded me that I lied about our road trip. He flipped between being hurt, upset, and angry. And I honestly think he was a little excited to go and tell Amanda the latest," Kate replied.

She hated confirming that he was a source all along. He had told Amanda everything. She felt betrayed by the person who was supposed to love her most.

"He also asked about you. Why are you my partner in crime? What is going on with us?" Her cheeks flushed at the suggestion there was something going on. "I, uh, told him we're friends. That you've believed me since the beginning." She felt breathless all of a sudden. "And how you've helped me with your vast knowledge of NASA and space. I emphasized that nothing else matters but the pledge and Rex right now. We're all in terrible danger. We need to stay focused and maybe, hopefully, save some people."

"That's probably for the best now—" Sinclair trailed off as numerous cars, trucks, and vans rumbled down the street. A few ominous black SUVs featured in the parade.

"I'm surprised it took them so long. Let's hurry and get inside," Sinclair said, taking the box out of Kate's arms and stacking it on top of the one he was holding. They rushed up the porch stairs.

Jo-Ellen opened the front door for them. "Perfect timing. Your first live interview starts in five minutes. I set up a place in the living room so you can sit on the couch and be comfortable," Jo-Ellen said, taking a box out of Sinclair's arms.

For three hours, Kate answered the same questions over and over. Some interviews were smoother than others. Often, the reporters would get emotional, angry, or sad when Kate admitted that she had no idea what kind of violence might happen or when.

"But can't you ask Rex? He speaks to you!" one anchor exclaimed with tears welling in her eyes.

"I can't make Rex communicate with me. I only know what I have told you. We are all on the same page with the same information now. We all have an important decision to make," Kate said over and over.

The questions shifted as the hours passed, as reporters and the public had time to really process the pledge and think more deeply about what was happening.

"That pledge is pretty intense. It's like you only want perfect people to go with Rex and live. What is that all about?" another anchor asked.

"A very smart woman that I met in jail yesterday said I should be careful to only bring good people, so that is what the pledge is also about. If a person wants to be the best person they can be, take responsibility for their actions, and commit to being kind, then this pledge provides the ability to express that to Rex and their fellow Earthlings, whom they may soon be living among in space. Remember, space will be very stressful because it will be very different. If people know they must be on their best behavior, well, I hope that relieves some stress for everyone," Kate explained.

"That woman must not be too smart if she's in jail," the anchor scoffed.

"We are living in such stressful times. The pandemic is crushing people with the fear of illness, disease, death, losing jobs, and maybe losing their homes. Then, on top of that, add the global mass shooting. So many people have lost loved ones. People do strange things when mourning and under pressure. The woman in jail did not hurt anyone. She was full of compassion. She worried about the people in space. She wanted them to be safe and not surrounded by bad people. That is also what the pledge is about—thinking about our compassion, empathy, and humanity," Kate replied.

There was another crash on the front door. All day, as the interviews were happening, people would knock on the door or slam into it with camera equipment. Impatient reporters would occasionally shout questions through the front window. Just when things seemed to be getting out of control, Amanda or another cop would clear the porch and the yard, yelling into bullhorns and threatening arrest.

A particularly loud bang made Kate jump. It was loud enough that the reporter heard it over the Zoom feed.

"Wow, this must be terrifying for you," the reporter said. "That almost sounded like gunshots. How are you holding up?"

"Thank you for asking. It has been a very stressful day, week, couple of months," Kate admitted, looking directly into the camera to speak to the people. "Please, everyone, read the pledge. Discuss it with your friends and loved ones. Really think deeply about it. There might not be a lot of time. I'm very sorry we are all going through this. Thank you for your attention—"

The reporter cut her off. "Well, it seems like fifty million people have decided to take a chance on you and Rex and space so far."

"What? How many? Sinclair, is that right?" Kate asked Sinclair, who was sitting in a comfortable chair just out off camera, staring at his laptop.

"That sounds right. Seems like Space Force is hosting it now and collecting signatures. Not sure when that happened or why," he replied.

"I have to go. Thank you so much for having me," Kate said quickly to the screen and snapped the laptop shut.

"It's working!" Kate said, standing and doing a little happy dance. "Jo-Ellen, I think my work is done. That was my last interview. People believe this is really happening. They believe me. They're signing the pledge! I think I'm done for the day."

"So, fifty million people have signed it in just six hours, since you first hit sent this morning. I agree: your work is done. It's spreading worldwide. It's all over the internet. Every news outlet everywhere is covering it," Sinclair said, his eyes on his computer screen.

"I'm so relieved! And so hungry!" Kate said, plopping back onto the couch.

"I'll start dinner. Jo-Ellen, I assume you're staying?" Sinclair asked as he peeled himself away from his computer and headed toward the kitchen.

"Yes. Of course, I am staying. Not sure I could leave anyway. I've been so busy keeping the interviews moving and Kate hydrated that I have not answered my phone," Jo-Ellen said, looking at her phone. "Space Force is freaking out. They're going to do a press conference at seven tonight. They want you, Kate. It will be interesting to learn why they are hosting the pledge."

"Nope. I'm done for the day. Also pretty much done with Space Force forever," Kate said.

Hopefully none of them dared to sign the pledge. Not after the way they have been treating us. No way I'm helping them with their PR mess.

Kate's phone rang. "I'm taking this," she said, heading through the kitchen to the back porch.

"Say hi to Jackie for me," Sinclair called as she walked by him.

"Will do!" Kate replied with a smile. "Hi, mom! How are you? Did you get my text?"

"Yes, I did. And I have been watching you all day on TV. You're doing a fantastic job! It's so exciting," Jackie replied.

"Mom, remember what my text said? Don't do anything until I tell you. This is serious, Mom. I know it's exciting but—" Before Kate could continue, her mom cut her off.

"I know, baby. I saw your text. I understand. That's not what I meant. What is so exciting is the—I don't know what to call it—explosions of kindness happening all over. It's like people want to prove they are worthy of the pledge, of Rex saving them, of you. It's just amazing."

"Huh? What are you talking about?" Kate asked.

"Go put on the news. See for yourself. Give Sinclair a hug for me. Call me later. I love you!" her mom said.

"Okay, will do, Mom. And remember—don't do anything until I text you. I love you too." Kate hung up and went to join the others.

"Here, take this. I'm going to make you a plate," Sinclair said, handing Kate a glass of wine as she entered the kitchen.

Kate took a sip. "Mom said I need to watch the news. Apparently, an explosion of random kindness is happening all around the world."

In the living room, Sinclair flipped from channel to channel. Kate's mother was right: people were uploading all kinds of actions to social media. There were small acts like helping the elderly with their groceries and big acts like saving a stranded baby elephant and reuniting it with its mother. Random trash pick-ups, school beautification projects, and charitable donations had skyrocketed. People talked about the July 14 orphans that they had taken in. Many people had been supportive of healthcare and frontline workers since the pandemic started in March, but this seemed different. It seemed more kind, authentic, and global. Everyone was wearing masks but seemed to be smiling with their eyes. Flipping from one happy story to the next, Kate laughed, while tears of happiness poured down her face.

"That's all you, Kate," Sinclair said as he reached for her hand.

TWENTY-THREE

Sixty-Two Days After the Shooting

Kate and Sinclair continued to watch the wonderful stories as they ate dinner.

Kate giggled and downed half a glass of wine. "This is so delicious. This food is so wonderful. I can't thank you enough, Sinclair," Kate gushed.

"It's just grilled vegetables with tofu. And you don't need to thank me, Kate. We are in this together. To the end," Sinclair said with a wink.

Kate's heart started thumping, and she felt her face turn hot.

Hopefully he thinks it's just the wine.

Jo-Ellen walked in the front door. Kate had almost forgotten she was still here since she had been outside on the phone for some time.

"Okay, lovebirds, what's for dinner?" Jo-Ellen asked, tossing her phone on the table. "I'm starving. And I need wine. What a frigging day, right?"

"My mom said we needed to watch TV," Kate said, flipping the channel to distract from the lovebird comment. "Look at this, Jo-Ellen."

"Am I seeing what I think I'm seeing?" Jo-Ellen asked. "Are you both seeing what I think we are seeing? People all over the world doing good deeds? Is this live, in real-time?" Jo-Ellen asked. "I don't understand."

"Yes, good deeds, and yes, in real-time," Sinclair murmured.

"I'm so amazed, stunned, impressed," Kate said. "People helping neighbors and planting crops and sharing their worldly possessions. Who would have thought we actually had this within us?"

Sinclair took the remote to flip through more channels. Sometimes, there seemed to be more reporters and press than actual do-gooders doing good. Despite losing 70 million people, America did not seem to lack reporters. Suddenly, a familiar face flashed across the screen. "Wait, stop. Don't flip. This story seems familiar," Kate shouted.

"I think that is the guy we heard interviewed on NPR on our drive. He was all alone in Montana or Idaho. Looks like hundreds of people have promised to move to his town and help hold it together. Remember that interview, Kate? We heard it while heading to Florida. He was so sad and pleading for help." Sinclair smiled. "It's such a weird coincidence that we caught that interview then, and here he is now, being interviewed again. He sounds relieved, almost happy."

"Definitely grateful," Kate said.

Sinclair brought out more food and wine.

They watched the CEO of a major oil company announce that they were donating $5 billion to put solar panels on low-income homes, schools, and non-profit businesses. He explained how to sign up through a website and asked the public to spread the word.

"I love this—watching people help each other. Watching them take real, meaningful action." Kate's eyes filled with tears again as she heard a woman explain how she had been adopting all the stray pets that had been wandering through her neighborhood since the shooting. She was feeding them and giving them shelter, and neighbors and news crews were jumping in to help.

"Three hundred million have signed the pledge. It's gone global," Jo-Ellen squealed.

"Damn! Three hundred million people have pledged to be the best they can be. That's pretty amazing," Sinclair said.

"I'm out of here, kids," Jo-Ellen said, getting up to leave. "Looks like the random acts of kindness have spread to your street. It's quiet out there. Hopefully, that means I can get home without any trouble. Anyway, I need to connect with some friends and family myself. I will be back in the morning."

And with her departure, Kate and Sinclair were alone.

TWENTY-FOUR

Sixty-Two Days After the Shooting

Sinclair locked the door behind Jo-Ellen and then muted the TV. "You did it again, Kate."

"Come on, Sinclair. You can't possibly be angry anymore," Kate said with a smile. "I gave everyone all the information. I have allowed them to make their own decision. Total free will. I know the pledge won't guarantee assholes don't get taken up, but at least it forces people to think. And it allows families to discuss the variables we can't control—"

"I was never really angry. But maybe I do owe you an apology," Sinclair interrupted. He reached for the wine bottle while Kate stood and held out her empty glass.

"You do?" Kate asked, feeling the heat rise from her feet up to her face, which she didn't know could blush hotter.

"I was an asshole about the pledge. I had a knee-jerk reaction. And I was wrong. You figured out a way to make it workable. I should never have doubted you. I'm sorry," Sinclair said.

"I accept your apology," Kate murmured. "I hate it when we aren't on the same page."

"Me too. I was being totally unfair," Sinclair said. "What I meant by 'you did it again' is that you were hit with some crazy, terrifying information and even went to jail, and in all that madness, you came up with the right thing to do. I'm sorry that I got in the way."

"It's okay, Sinclair," Kate said as he stared intensely into her eyes. Kate fought the desire to look away.

"No, it's not," Sinclair insisted

"Sinclair, you have helped me every step of the way! You believed this unreal story from the very beginning. You put your life in danger to help me. You've even been to the white room with me! So, we got frustrated with each other! We're all good now, okay?" Kate asked. "I mean, I know you're intrigued with extraterrestrials and it's why you got involved, but for whatever reason, you have been with me every step of the way on this terrifying adventure, and I'm extremely grateful."

Kate knew he joined the adventure for the potential fulfillment of a lifelong dream to encounter otherworldly life, but she hoped now he stayed in it for her.

"I don't think you understand how amazing you are. I'm grateful that Rex figured it out and picked you," Sinclair said.

Kate dropped her chin, unable to meet Sinclair's eyes. Everything about him was sexy. His beautiful, soulful eyes, his brilliant brain, his muscular body. She couldn't hide her attraction any longer.

"Have you signed the pledge?" Sinclair asked.

Kate started pacing, avoiding eye contact. "Not yet," she replied.

"Why not?" He walked closer to her.

Heat exploded all over Kate's body. She thought of all the times she had just casually hugged him, reaching for him for comfort.

If we touch now, he'll feel the heat and know how much I want him.

She backed away.

Sinclair just moved closer. "Look at me, Kate. Why haven't you signed your pledge yet?"

Kate sighed, stopped moving, and looked him right in the eyes. "I haven't signed the pledge yet because—" She took a deep breath in.

"Because?" He tucked a strand of hair behind her red-hot ear.

"Because I was waiting to see if you were going to sign too. Sinclair, I don't want to go into space without you. I like being with you. I want to be with you. Here or there."

Sinclair took her face in his hands and stared into her eyes. Before she knew it, his lips were on hers, a sweet kiss that quickly grew intense, hard, and passionate.

Butterflies erupted all over her body. She pressed herself closer to him, the need to touch him everywhere now undeniable. As their tongues seem to wrestle for dominance, they pulled off each other's shirts. As Kate reached for Sinclair's jeans zipper, he grabbed her hand and quickly led her up the stairs. Kate giggled the whole way up.

So, this is happening? Her heart beat fast. *This is really happening. I need to stop laughing. There is nothing sexy about giggling.*

The thought made her laugh even more.

In his room, she jumped onto Sinclair's bed and reached for him, pulling him down to join her.

Whether he signs the pledge or not, I have no intention of ever leaving his side. Together 'til the end. Whenever and however it comes.

TWENTY-FIVE

Sixty-Three Days After
the Shooting

A pounding on the door jerked them both awake. Sinclair bolted up to a sitting position.

Waking up naked in Sinclair's bed, Kate was suddenly shy, especially thinking about all the things they had done to each other the night before.

"I don't care who it is. I'm not getting it. We're sleeping in," Sinclair said, reaching for his phone and tossing it on the floor. "It's not even eight yet. So rude." He laid back down and pulled Kate onto his chest.

His phone started buzzing.

"Seriously. I may never get out of this bed. Just turn it off. Mine's off," Kate mumbled, snuggling into Sinclair's chest, the thump-thump of his heart against her hand, lulling her to sleep.

They hadn't gotten much sleep.

After a few minutes, his phone went off loudly and the knocking started up again.

"Dammit." He reached for his phone on the floor and read the texts. "It's Jo-Ellen. Over one billion people have signed the pledge. All the networks want to talk to you."

Kate yawned, reluctant to leave Sinclair's bed, the place where she felt so peaceful and warm and satiated. She did not want to think about death or the pledge. She stretched and realized she was not totally satiated. She'd love to relive every moment of the last eight hours.

"I want nothing more than to stay in bed with you all day." Sinclair pulled her on top of him. "We deserve a day off from saving the world."

She kissed his soft lips. "Well, now that we're awake—" She trailed kisses along his strong jawline, playing with his earlobe. Kate squealed when he flipped her over and laid down on her. Their bodies fit together perfectly.

It was close to noon when Kate got out of bed, feeling fully awake and ready to start the day. She walked to the bathroom completely nude.

She'd never been so happy in her life. Sinclair was fantastic and the most skilled lover she'd ever been with. The intensity of their connection gave her a sense of comfort and confidence.

Shit. What will I tell Kyle? Maybe I don't deserve to sign my own pledge!

Kate started to quietly dress but still woke Sinclair up.

"I thought we were staying in bed today," Sinclair said as he stretched his arms overhead and gave her a lazy, sleepy smile. "Jo-Ellen is not the boss. We can get back to her and the press when we want to."

"I agree, Jo-Ellen is not the boss, but Rex is," Kate said, quickly pulling on her shorts and bra, remembering her shirt was downstairs.

"Are you upset? You seem upset. Tell me what you are thinking, Kate. Slow down and let's talk."

Kate grabbed one of Sinclair's folded t-shirts from a stack on a chair and threw it over her head. It smelled like him, igniting her arousal again. But she couldn't be half-naked for this conversation.

Kate sat on the bed and looked at Sinclair. "Last night, I told you I had not signed the pledge because I was waiting to see if you did. I honestly don't want to go to space without you. I mean it. If you choose to stay here, so will I."

"I know, Kate. I feel the same. We stick together," he said, taking her hand and bringing it to his mouth to kiss.

"But now, I can't sign it, even if you decide to," Kate said. "I feel like a hypocrite. The pledge is about being honest and good and thoughtful. What am I going to tell Kyle? I betrayed him. I told him there was nothing but friendship between us, which I guess was the truth yesterday, but not really entirely the truth. I feel guilty. I'm being selfish."

"You aren't being selfish," Sinclair insisted. "You moved your stuff out. He betrayed you when he told Amanda things you clearly asked him not to discuss with anyone. He might be with her now. But if you're feeling guilty for what we did, well, just know I don't feel guilty for any of it."

"Things are just really complicated and confusing," Kate admitted as the events of the past two months flew through her mind.

"I guess, on paper, I should be feeling guilty as well. Yvette has only been gone for a couple of months," Sinclair muttered.

Kate's heart flipped.

I have been so selfish! I have not given Yvette and Sinclair as a couple a thought!

"I'm sorry, Sinclair—"

"Don't be, Kate. Yvette and I were separating, as I told you. We had been growing apart for some time. But most people don't know that, and on paper, it looks like you and I moved fast. But these are extreme times with extreme circumstances, and I don't feel guilty at all and you shouldn't either," Sinclair said, squeezing her hand.

They both jumped as a loud banging started on the front door again.

"Jesus. What's wrong with people!" Sinclair groaned as he hopped out of bed and started to quickly dress. "Look, Kate, we are living in extraordinary times. Maybe you and Kyle didn't exactly get closure or officially break things off. I want to give you space to do what you need to do to feel like you did right by him. And from the little I know of him, I think Kyle will understand. We will get through this together," Sinclair said, pulling Kate in for a hug.

"Or we won't. It's all up to Rex and the others," Kate said with a chill running down her spine. Memories of July 14 flashed through her mind.

They both jumped again as they heard the back-door open and close.

"What the hell! That was locked." Sinclair rushed out of the bedroom and down the stairs.

Kate turned on her phone, which blew up with text notifications and breaking news announcements. She sighed and turned it off. She sat back down on the bed and shut her eyes, taking a few deep medita-tive breaths.

I will worry about the rest of the world later. I want to enjoy these moments with Sinclair and savor this rela-tionship. After all, we have no idea what will happen next.

Feeling better, she went down the stairs. "I hope whoever broke in brought food because I'm starving!" she called.

She stopped dead when she saw the look in Kyle's eyes.

Oh. It wasn't Jo-Ellen.

Why would he barge into a locked house?

The nerve of him.

"Hey, Kyle. What's up? How did you get in? I mean, whatever, that's not really important. What's up?" Kate asked again, hearing the nerves rattle in her own voice.

"I was worried when I couldn't get a hold of either of you. I was afraid you had been arrested again or abducted or a mob got you or something, so I broke the back door!" Kyle snapped, flushing red with anger.

"Oh, *now* you're worried I was arrested! Too bad that thought didn't occur to you when you got your girlfriend to call in a tip about me!" Kate responded, equally irate.

Kyle shifted his glare to Sinclair. "I tried contacting you for hours." He emphasized the word *hours* with a menacing tone Kate had never heard from him before. "Amanda was worried too and encouraged me to come over here and see if you were okay."

Kate winced. Kyle was generally a great guy and his concern was very considerate.

"You could have been dead. But I'm not stupid, my worry was for naught. Seems like you guys were just messing around. Sleeping in together," Kyle said, his flushed face and angry glare directed back at Kate.

Kate was speechless.

She glanced at Sinclair who had moved far enough away to provide a little space but close enough to join the conversation if needed.

"Kyle, thanks for your concern. It was not unfounded during these scary and bizarre times. Obviously, you and I have grown apart and moved in different directions. Last night, we turned off our phones because they just don't stop ringing and … and … and I'm sorry," Kate managed, tears filling her eyes.

"That's it? That's all you have to say?" Kyle asked, eyes tearing up too.

Sinclair walked quietly into the kitchen.

"I'm so sorry, Kyle. I don't know when it happened. When I started to have feelings for Sinclair. This is brand new. I know that doesn't make a difference, really. It just happened. I'm so sorry," Kate said as she wiped away the tears rolling down her cheeks. Even though it was the right thing to do, Kate felt wretched breaking up with Kyle. She never wanted to hurt him. She didn't blame him either; everyone's behavior had changed since the shooting.

Kyle backed up, putting more space between them, and blinked away his tears. "Whatever. I'm not really surprised. Amanda said there was something going on between you two all along. I came to tell you that reporters were asking to interview me, as your boy-friend. I guess to corroborate your story and role in all this and get a personal perspective on you, Kate, the *hero* of the world," he said, snidely. "I have no desire to do so. Maybe they should interview Sinclair? He can say how he seduced you, maybe took advan-tage of you, during a highly stressful time."

"It's not like that, Kyle. It just happened. But maybe, in a way, you're right. We grew close fast because we have been in this crazy shitstorm together. I don't know—"

"I'm leaving. I will not be doing any interviews. Please ask the media to stop bothering me. Tell them I am no longer your boyfriend," Kyle said as he stomped toward the broken door.

"Wait, Kyle. Did you sign the pledge?" Kate called to his departing back.

"It's none of your goddamn business," Kyle shouted over his shoulder.

"I get it. You're right. It's none of my business. I just want you to make a decision fast. Today is the fifth day since my last encounter with Rex. The violence could start anytime," Kate explained quickly.

"What the hell? That is a huge point *not* to have discussed with us or in the dozens of interviews yesterday! Jesus, you did not mention a hard deadline once!" Jo-Ellen said as she entered the kitchen through the broken back door. "What happened here?" She glanced down at the broken glass on the floor.

Kyle swung the door wider so he could pass through without touching Jo-Ellen and stomped down the steps, across the small yard, and toward the fence gate.

"Oh, that doesn't matter," Kate said as she wiped tears off her cheeks. "Kyle and I just broke up."

TWENTY-SIX

Sixty-Three Days After the Shooting

Jo-Ellen looked Kate up and down. Kate felt disheveled with her messy bedhead and Sinclair's way too large t-shirt.

"It's about time," Jo-Ellen remarked. "I had my money on you guys hooking up two weeks ago."

Kate and Sinclair looked at each other but didn't say anything.

"And I'm happy for you. Trust me, I am. But I've called and texted and had no choice but to come over because I got no response from either of you. I know you're in love, but we still have a crisis to contend with."

"I'll be right back," Kate said as she rushed through the broken door and down the steps. She needed Kyle to know he had to make his choice regardless of how he felt about her.

"Wait! Kyle! Hang on. Come back!" Kate yelled at the swinging gate Kyle had just passed through.

She pulled it open, went through, and then *swoosh*. She was flying through space with such speed that her stomach entered her mouth.

She hit the weird white floor with more force than before. On her hands and knees, she gasped for air while bile shot out of her mouth.

She squeezed into a ball on the floor, circling her arms around her bare knees. Her teeth chattered so hard she feared she would break them. She recalled she was wearing Sinclair's shirt which was far too large for her, so she pulled her arms in the holes and put her knees into the shirt. Anything to get warm. It seemed to be taking longer than normal to warm up.

Sinclair! Is he here too?

Kate tried to look around, but it was just too cold. She had to focus on not freezing to death.

Will space feel like this? So painfully cold that I will not want to move?

After a few minutes, she could feel warmth seeping into her bones. She pulled her limbs out, putting the shirt back correctly. She thought it must feel colder because she was only wearing shorts, a bra, and a t-shirt; she usually had on a few more articles of clothing, like shoes and socks.

Does the heat come from inside or outside?

She also wondered if she only now considered where the heat came from because this might soon be her new home.

"R-R-R-R-Rex, I h-h-ave s-s-s-so m-m-many questions. Thanks for g-g-rab-b-b-ing m-m-me," Kate managed through chattering teeth.

When it was warm enough for Kate to stand, she looked around for Sinclair, disappointed to see he didn't come up with her.

"Rex? Rex? Are you here?" Kate cried out, realizing Rex was not there either.

The room was silent.

Kate moved around, touching the white walls and floor.

Where the hell is Rex? Shit! I hope the others did not do something to him!

"I'm here, Kate," Rex said in his slow cadence.

Kate jumped and spun around. There was Rex in his normal place and normal position.

"Oh, thank God! I worried something had happened to you! What's going on?" Kate asked.

"Kate. We don't have time. The others are coming," Rex warned.

"I know they are coming! They're coming to hurt us. I am very well aware. I have questions about your offer to bring other people up here, to avoid violence. How many people can you bring up? Will they be safe, Rex? Will you hurt them? Us? What will it be like up here? Do you think you could bring up a billion people? What about their pets? Is that too much to ask?" Kate asked, wincing at the enormous request.

"Kate. We don't have time. I will let you know when they are here. You've tried. You have done so much. All I can do now is let you know when they are here," Rex said.

"Wait. Why can't we talk for a minute? Please. Please, Rex, I need some answers. What will the others do?" Kate asked. "Can we stop them?" When she paused for an answer, she felt the floor buckle beneath her feet.

"No, Rex!" Kate screamed as she felt the rush.

She landed hard on Sinclair's bed. So hard that she almost bounced off.

She laid her head on the pillow. Tears of frustration rolled down her cheeks, but she snapped up when she heard Sinclair's voice downstairs.

"I checked the back alley and ran across the street. I don't see her anywhere!" Sinclair shouted as he ran up the stairs.

"Did you talk to Kyle?" Jo-Ellen called up to him.

"No. That's not a good idea," Sinclair yelled over his shoulder.

"I'm here!" Kate called from the bed.

Sinclair burst into the room and ran over to the bed, pulling her into his arms.

"How did you get upstairs?" Jo-Ellen asked, poking her head in.

"Rex," Sinclair answered, squeezing tighter. "Are you okay?" he asked, his lips pressed against the top of her head.

Kate just nodded into his chest.

"What did he say?"

Kate pulled out of his embrace. "Very little. I asked several questions but got no answers. All he said was the others are coming, we don't have time, and he'll let me know when they arrive. He also said he knew we tried. That we have done so much. Not sure what any of it means."

She stood up from the bed and looked from Sinclair's worried face to Jo-Ellen's.

"I asked him how many people he could take up. I asked if they—*we*—would be okay, safe. He did not answer," Kate said. "I didn't have time to explain the pledge."

The room was silent until Kate's stomach growled very loudly.

Jo-Ellen laughed. "Good thing he did not keep you long! You may have gotten hangry and said something you would regret. You'd lose your spot on the Ark."

"Okay. You need food. And we have some time, right? He said the others were coming, so they aren't here yet. That's good," Sinclair said. "Though, why would he pull you up just to say that? I mean, we knew they were coming. That's not exactly new information."

"Maybe because today is the deadline. Right, Kate? Isn't that what you were telling Kyle when I arrived?" Jo-Ellen asked.

"There was a deadline, Kate?" Sinclair asked.

"Not really. I think I sarcastically asked, 'when? In five days?' when Rex pulled me up from the beach because that is what he always said before. He did not confirm. Just said soon. But it has now been five days so everyone needs to make their decision, just in case. Of course, we don't know if Rex will take everyone. The pledge could be useless. Where are we now? How many have signed it?" Kate asked.

Jo-Ellen looked at her phone. "Like I texted earlier, over a billion. More than one billion people have signed your pledge. One of the big newspapers said they were looking at all the signers and would have an official number soon, then would run a clock. Like the

COVID death clock. People are really into it. It's the cool thing to do and trending hard. Well, the pledge and doing good deeds. All your interviews yesterday convinced people to sign it."

"My intention was not to convince them they had to or should sign it. I just wanted to explain the situation clearly and give them the information." Kate sighed, feeling like a failure. "What if, after all of that, it doesn't even work?"

People will be angry. Angry mobs will surely come after me. Well, if they aren't all dead.

TWENTY-SEVEN

Sixty-Three Days After the Shooting

An hour later, Kate sat on Sinclair's couch, properly cleaned, clothed, and fed. The TV was on and the news continued to show amazing explosions of kindness, as Kate's mom called them. They were highlighting more people that opened their doors to the orphans from July 14. Under normal circumstances, Kate would probably cry happy tears that people were looking after these kids permanently. It was such a big commitment to raise other people's children. But she could not focus on the news.

She wanted Jo-Ellen to leave. She wanted to talk to Sinclair. Kiss Sinclair. Talk about Kyle. What had she done? She'd hurt Kyle. She knew he had not trusted her or believed her throughout this whole ordeal, but it was *Kyle*. It had been fantastic once, but not since the mass shooting. She knew breaking-up was the right thing, but she felt sad anyway.

"What are you thinking?" Sinclair asked, sitting down on the couch beside her.

"Not about the others and our impending doom. Not about the pledge. I honestly think I have done all I can for Rex and the others," Kate said.

Sinclair looked into her eyes. "It's okay to think about other things. Maybe try to think about happy things?"

"Okay, lovebirds, you're going to enjoy this!" Jo-Ellen interrupted, plopping down on the couch. She grabbed the remote and changed the channel. "The Speaker is doing a joint press conference with the President."

"We are all under a great deal of stress about this 'I Chose to Live in Space, Rather Than Die on Earth Pledge.' We have heard from Kate Stellute through the media. She did numerous interviews. We have heard from Space Force and the Department of Justice. It's a personal choice to sign the pledge. Every American, talking with their family and loved ones, must make the choice," the Speaker said into a microphone, through a mask that read *be kind*. "The government is not making this choice for anyone. Congress is not making a recommendation one way or the other. It's a personal, individual choice."

"Looks like they are outside the Capitol. So ridiculous—she is wearing a mask but he isn't. I mean, sure, we may all die today or go into space, but do we really want COVID in space?" Kate asked. "That would totally suck—to survive the violence here, just to die of COVID up there."

"Shush," Jo-Ellen said.

The President leaned over the Speaker and said into the microphone, "But I do not intend to sign it. Is it legally binding? Who knows! What are the consequences if you break the pledge? Who knows! My lawyers have advised me not to sign it and I won't. Come on. Rex killed hundreds of millions of people on July 14, and we should trust him? I will not sign it. At least, not yet."

Good, Kate thought. She didn't want that liar in space. She had no faith that he could keep the pledge even if he signed it.

The Speaker rolled her eyes. "It's a complicated personal choice. Anyway, we are here to share some great news with the American public. As everyone knows, we lost a lot of members of Congress on July 14. We lost a lot of people in the administration and throughout the government, but those of us that are still here have decided to reimagine America. Do things that need to be done. Solve problems that have languished due to partisan bickering. Things that seemed too hard for far too long, while the status quo was just too easy. But after losing so much, we have decided to trust science and each other to create a better America."

The Majority Leader of the Senate stepped up to the microphone beside the Speaker. The Members of Congress in attendance and the President shifted around, all angling to be on camera.

Do they really even understand what it means to be good and selfless? They are politicians.

"Congress passed several bills yesterday. Bills that had previously been passed by the House or Senate, but got bogged down by politics, lobbyists, and corporate greed, that put selfish dangerous behavior above the needs of the American people. In an unprecedented move, the President came here, to the Capitol, to sign these bills into law," the Senate Leader explained.

The Speaker took back the microphone.

"She's so tough. I love her. Look at these men trying to box her out. Idiots," Jo-Ellen murmured.

"Shush," Kate said, smiling.

"The legislation includes a climate bill that will immediately put a high enough tax on carbon emissions to make alternative energy cost-effective right now, not ten years in the future, while oil companies make billions and continue to destroy the planet. We are simply making oil and gas companies internalize their externalities, meaning the cost of carbon-based oil and fuel will include the cost of cleaning up oil spills, proper and safe disposal of coal ash, and resiliency against extreme weather damage, as well as helping cover costs to those that have lost so much already." The Speaker paused as some reporters cheered and clapped.

The Senate Leader leaned in. "We are also revoking the billions in tax breaks the oil industry has been receiving for over a century. Those funds will go to putting solar panels on roofs across America. As we address the huge changes to America as a result of losing 70 million people and reimagine a new future, we have to do things right, for our people and planet."

Kate couldn't contain her glee and did a little excited dance with her hands.

"One bill provides for universal healthcare for all Americans. We have learned during a pandemic and mass shooting that we are all in this together. The disease, death, and destruction impacted the insured as much as the uninsured, and we all share the same hospitals and medical staff. We lost so many people in the medical industry. We need a system that works together, seamlessly, and does not waste time figuring out how much money each insurance company and pharmaceutical company will receive. It was fun for so many companies and CEOs that got very, very rich, but that party is over. We know our current system is complicated, unfair, unsustainable, and does not work for the American public, and today, we are changing it," the Speaker continued, having taken back the microphone. More applause interrupted her.

Sinclair stood up and joined in the applause. "Did you hear that? Universal healthcare!"

"It's almost too good to be true," Jo-Ellen said, clapping enthusiastically.

Kate was stunned into silence. *Climate change. Healthcare. What else is in this legislative dream package and how the hell did they convince this terrible President to sign them?*

"Another bill creates paid leave for all working Americans that need time off work due to illness or other life emergencies. It also includes a new mandatory minimum wage to help us try to balance the income inequality this country has been experiencing. And, perhaps most importantly, the final bill requires companies to pay for and manage all pollution and waste. That includes chemical waste from manufacturing processes, animal waste from factory farms, and fertilizer runoff that destroys our rivers, waterways, and oceans. If a product uses or comes in plastic, the corporation must safely recycle or dispose of it, and if they can't, they can't produce it or use it. And this, of course, includes waste in space. If NASA or private space exploration can't manage and safely remove their debris, they can't go into space," the Speaker said. "Of course, we cannot control what is produced in other countries, but we do hope that other nations will soon follow suit with their own legislation. Those that don't, well, we won't be doing business with them anymore."

Reporters and people watching the press conference started to cheer. The sustained applause went on for a couple of minutes. Kate looked at Jo-Ellen and Sinclair; their smiles were beaming.

"This is all you, Kate," Sinclair said, with a wink.

The President snatched the microphone. "I'm sorry. I just have to say something. These bogus, socialist-inspired bills will make everything more expensive. Think the CEOs will take a pay cut? Ha! Think again. Products will be more expensive. Sorry, people, the nanny state wants you to be able to buy less! How un-American."

"Be still my heart. Is this possible? Is this true?" Kate asked, ignoring the President's dire fearmongering. "I feel like I'm in a dream!"

"Fuck the greedy CEOs. Well, those that did not die on July 14. The world has changed. They are no longer in control and we all need to consume less,"

Sinclair said. "These bills—I mean, laws—sound wonderful. Creating nirvana, here on Earth!"

"Shush!" Jo-Ellen said, smiling.

The Senate Leader took the microphone. "Look, we lost 70 million Americans in one day because of our irresponsible behavior. We have all lost someone. But even before the mass shooting, we were destroying our oceans and atmosphere. We were driving species to extinction with our pollution. Our addiction to plastic everything was poisoning wildlife. Excessive fertilizer use was causing deadly red tides and algae blooms. We destroyed so much natural habitat for, what, more cheap beef? Our actions exploited and abused animals and caused this horrible coronavirus pandemic that has killed hundreds of thousands of Americans. We are killing ourselves. We refused to talk about it or acknowledge it, but it has to stop. And yes, this legislation curtails corporations from causing deadly pollution, but we must acknowledge that we buy their products, and we created the financial incentive for them to pollute every time we made a purchase. We are all part of the problem and we must all be part of the solution."

"We are not blaming corporate America. We love rich people. I love rich people. I'm one of the richest men in America. We all know it. These bills are an incentive for us to all work together to do things better and safer and still make money. I lost three kids on July 14. We need to clean up our pollution," the President added, seeming to be back on message.

"I can't believe this is happening! This is so awesome!" Kate said. "I'm impressed that the biodiversity extinction crisis was included. People often forget how important wildlife and plants are. They see nature as something for fun or to be used but not necessary for life."

"Wildlife, plants, and nature will benefit from many of these bills, and sadly, a smaller human population, Kate. But it's all good," Sinclair said, still smiling from ear to ear.

"Yes, awesome. But it does seem too good to be true. We'd better read those bills before we celebrate. The devil is always in the details. Like they might seem like great bills but may not include enforcement or just require useless reports and grants but no meaningful change. It's still the US Congress and this douche President," Jo-Ellen said. "You can't trust politicians."

"Trust, but verify," Sinclair added while nodding his head.

There was a flurry of movement as the President signed page after page. As he did so, reporters shouted out questions.

"Mr. President, did you sign the pledge?"

"Madam Speaker, do you recommend that Americans sign the pledge?"

Kate clicked off the TV. "I don't want to hear about the pledge anymore. Let's just be happy they passed those bills."

"Agree! Let's open a bottle of something and celebrate!" Jo-Ellen said. "What do you have that's really good and really expensive, Sinclair?"

Sinclair flashed Kate a look that made her melt inside. "This seems the perfect time for a bottle of champagne I've been saving for a special occasion. And today, well, today is one of the best days of my life."

Kate smiled at him; she couldn't wait to get him back into bed.

TWENTY-EIGHT

Sixty-Three Days After the Shooting

A s they laughed and enjoyed the delicious champagne, Jo-Ellen called for a toast. "You did it again, Kate! Kate saved the world AGAIN! To Kate!"

"Yes, to Kate!" Sinclair agreed, clinking glasses.

"We all did it, working together!" Kate laughed.

This was fun but Kate really wanted Jo-Ellen to leave. The champagne was going to her head, and she was ready to lose herself in kissing Sinclair. They hadn't kissed since they got out of bed that morning. She really wanted to be alone with him.

"Hey, guys, I think I am going to go for a run. Just a few miles in the park. I need to clear my head and think. This is fun, but we are not out of danger," Kate said.

Jo-Ellen hates running. Please take a hint and go home.

"I should go with you, otherwise I'll worry. Is it okay if I run with you?" Sinclair winked as he asked.

"Sure," Kate said.

Jo-Ellen looked at her phone. "So many reporters want to speak to you. Space Force has called several times. I'm not going. I don't run or drive when drinking. Okay, I don't ever run unless I have to. I might order a pizza. You go, have fun. I'll get a vegan one for when you get back." As her phone rang, Jo-Ellen hurried into the kitchen.

Sinclair and Kate went upstairs to change into running clothes. As soon as the bedroom door closed, Sinclair pulled Kate into his arms.

"I have wanted to kiss you all day," he said while pressing his lips into her neck, his breath hot and electrifying.

"Me too! Jo-Ellen can't take a hint," Kate said as Sinclair planted irresistible kisses around her neck and ears.

Within seconds, they'd undressed. Sinclair pushed her onto the bed and they quickly found each other, found the rhythm that left Kate breathless.

When they were done, Kate giggled. "We should have been quieter. Don't want Jo-Ellen to hear," she whispered.

Just then, they heard Jo-Ellen burst into loud laughter downstairs, followed by another *pop*.

"She's having fun. She's talking to someone and drinking my champagne. I'm not going to worry if she hears us," Sinclair said as he kissed Kate's tummy and headed farther down

An hour later, still naked in bed, they heard a knock on the front door.

"Jo-Ellen's pizza has arrived. Let's sneak out while she's preoccupied," Sinclair said.

They quickly dressed and quietly went downstairs. Slipping past the front door, they could hear Jo-Ellen talking to someone on the front porch, laughing and offering them champagne. They quickly ran through the living room, kitchen, and out the back door.

Kate chuckled as they hustled down the street and into the park. "I feel like I'm back in high school and sneaking out."

"I doubt she knows what we were doing. She probably thinks we left a long time ago and are on a really long run. She's been drinking for a couple of hours," Sinclair said.

They walked to a clearing near some picnic tables. It was early evening and the sky was blue.

"I'm too tired to actually run. Can we sit?" Kate asked as she climbed up on the table and sat cross-legged. "Now that I think about it, what is Jo-Ellen's MO? She knows something is going on between us. I mean, we are all friends now and work together, but she has been staying extra close. Don't you think?"

"She loved helping destroy the debris. She seems to really enjoy being your communications director and helping get the pledge out in the world. She loved that press conference. I know this is all life-or-death constant drama, but I think she's just happy to be part of it all. I guess it's better to be in it rather than at her condo wondering what is going on. I would feel that way," Sinclair said.

"Yes, that makes sense." Kate was still suspicious, especially given that Space Force was still Jo-Ellen's employer. "I guess I'm still a little mistrustful. Not that long ago, she was paid to report our movements to Space Force."

"Let's not worry about her," Sinclair said as he laid down on the table and looked up at the sky. "It's a gorgeous fall evening. Let's just take a minute and enjoy this."

Kate smiled and laid back next to him. She put one hand under her head as a pillow and reached for Sinclair's with the other.

He squeezed it and brought it to his mouth for a quick kiss.

"I don't want to live anywhere that doesn't have fluffy clouds, oak trees, grass meadows, moths, squirrels, cicadas, crickets, and starlings," Kate said, admiring her surroundings. "I love this park."

"Kate, we need to decide if we're going to sign the pledge. Are we going or are we staying? I will do whatever you want. I just want to be with you," Sinclair said. "We have been through this crazy adventure together, and I have learned that you are the most kind, most compassionate, and yes, definitely the bravest person I have ever met. Rex has chosen wisely."

Sinclair's words reminded Kate of the story Rex told her—why he chose her. She hadn't shared it with Sinclair yet; there had not been time, or a right time, to go into it.

Kate brought Sinclair's hand to her mouth and kissed it.

"I could never have done any of this without you. None of it. We saved humanity, well, what is left of it, for a little while anyway. And I know I say I don't want to live where there's no nature or wild things, but I think I want to see where this goes. How it ends. Plus, we wrote the pledge. I think we should sign it. But I won't without you." Kate turned her face toward Sinclair's. "I just want to be with you."

Without sitting up, Sinclair took his phone out of his pocket and pulled up the pledge. With a few clicks, it was done. He signed the pledge.

Kate took her phone out of her pocket and did the same.

Some squirrels bickered loudly in a tree behind them.

Kate sighed. "I wish we could stay here without dying. That would be ideal. I would love to see a world that actually stops climate change. I want to see the oceans full of frolicking dolphins and whales. I want to go down to Florida and try and count the sea turtles and manatees but have to give up because there are so many. I want to see kids swimming in the lagoon beside them! Hell, I want to see kids playing in the Anacostia River because it's safe and clean. I want to see the skies darken with birds and wildlife abounding everywhere, the way it should be," Kate mused. Sinclair squeezed her hand.

"The way it could be without pollution," he said.

"I want people to be happy and make better choices because they are valued and paid fairly and have healthcare and live in a healthy environment. We are all connected. I want a world where people value that connection," Kate said. "People sometimes make terrible choices to be safe. Maybe Rex has taught us we should make good, loving, sustainable decisions at all times because being safe is a false concept. Our safety is so easily manipulated."

"But a lot of the choices are just selfish. It will be very interesting to see what happens in space if Rex pulls us all up. Maybe he will just pick a few. We really have no idea what will happen," Sinclair said.

"Oh, that reminds me. I need to text my mom." Kate pulled her phone out again.

"Mom, sign the pledge. We just did. Here is the link. Send," Kate said out loud as she texted. "She was waiting to do what I did and I told her I needed to find out what you wanted. We are all connected!" She laughed, feeling happy, relaxed, and resolved.

A couple of squirrels ran around the picnic table, chasing each other. Some loud birds flew overhead, squawking.

I wish it would just stay like this forever. Me and Sinclair, together, lounging on a picnic table in my favorite park on this amazing planet.

"I'm going to miss angry birds, silly squirrels, and clouds. I love watching… holy shit! Sinclair, do you see that?" Kate asked, shooting up to a seated position. Sinclair did the same.

The puffy evening clouds formed menacing words: "THEY'RE HERE."

TWENTY-NINE

Sixty-Three Days After the Shooting

Kate and Sinclair stared up at the clouds.

"Wow, I guess they're here. I hadn't anticipated such a clear warning. I guess it's a warning, right?" Kate asked. "Geez, my heart is pounding out of my chest!"

"I suppose so," Sinclair responded, laying back down on the table. "What can we do, Kate? It's a beautiful evening. We're in a pretty park. We've done all we can. You've done all you can do."

"Yes, I guess you're right," Kate said, taking a loud, deep breath and laying back down. "Do you think everyone can see this? This strange, terrifying message in the clouds?"

Kate's phone started to ring.

"Hi, Mom. Where are you?" Kate asked. "You're on the beach with Lourdes and friends? That sounds great! With margaritas, even better! Can you see it? In the clouds?"

Kate just nodded her head, listening to her mother.

"Yep. Sinclair and I are in a great spot. You're saying the same thing Sinclair just did. We've done all we can. We did our best. I'm happy you're having fun on the beach right now. It's perfect," Kate said into the phone.

She hoped she'd see her mom wherever they went next.

"I love you too. You have been the best mother in the world. Thank you for everything. I hope to see you soon," Kate said. Tears streamed out of her eyes as she hung up.

Sinclair sat up and made phone calls. Kate could hear his half of the conversations. First, he called his parents and then, Karisma. He said similar things to what Kate had just said to her mother.

"I'm turning off my phone. Everything that needed to be said has been said," Sinclair finally said, powering it off. He laid back down, taking Kate's hand again.

"You've been all over the world. Where would you want to spend your last moments on Earth alive? Rome? Paris? Madrid? Texas?" Kate asked.

"You've traveled some as well. What about you? The Caribbean? Argentina? Florida?" Sinclair asked.

"We have led extraordinary lives, even if they seemed common while actually living them. We survived a global mass shooting and a global pandemic, so far anyway," Kate said, wiping away her tears. "We are very, very lucky."

"And we got to meet Rex. Extraordinary lives indeed," Sinclair agreed. "But if I am going to die today or leave Earth forever, this is exactly where I want to be. You are the person I want to be with. I love you, Kate. You came out of nowhere, changed my life, and took me on this incredible adventure, and I thank you for that. And I really do love you. I'm not just saying that because we are most likely about to die," Sinclair said with a laugh.

"I love you too. Thank you for helping me with this, well, all of this. I couldn't have done it without you." Kate took his hand and pressed it to her heart.

They held hands on the table as the sun went down, gazing at the threatening clouds.

THIRTY

Sixty-Three Days After the Shooting

"I think we should head home. My back is getting stiff, and I am being eaten alive by mosquitoes," Kate said as she slapped one on her arm.

"This has been kind of anti-climactic. Wonder what's going on?" Sinclair asked.

They walked slowly back to Sinclair's, holding hands. On their street, they found a mob of reporters. Cars and vans lined the street. Kyle was standing on his front porch. He looked relieved when he saw Kate. They waved at each other.

"There she is—Kate Stellute!" A reporter yelled as she and her camera person ran toward Kate.

A crowd gathered around them. They shouted questions from every direction:

"Have you been in space?"

"Have you talked to Rex?"

"What did he say?"

"What does the message mean?"

"When will he pick us up? The people that signed the pledge."

"How long until there is more violence? Until we die?"

The last question caused a commotion and Kate found herself being shoved. A microphone was pushed into her face and hit her mouth so hard that her lip started bleeding.

"Come on, people! Did any of you sign the pledge? This is not acceptable behavior!" Kate shouted. "I know we're all scared. If you're not having an anxiety attack about now, I question your sanity. But that does not make it okay to hurt and scare people. Please back up and I will respond to your questions!"

The reporters backed up, many mumbling, "I'm sorry." They even apologized to other reporters that, a moment ago, they were pushing out of the way. They moved enough to create a path for Kate.

Kate started walking slowly toward Sinclair's house. A hand from the crowd handed her a bullhorn—her bullhorn. She recognized her handwriting on it. She flipped it on and said, "Thanks, Kyle!" so loud that, many people, including Sinclair, jumped in surprise.

"I know we are all scared. Terrified. Are we waiting to die? Will it be fast? A nuclear bomb? Raging fires that consume everything? Floods? Yes, I have imagined all the worst-case scenarios as well. Or are we waiting to leave Earth? Did the pledge work? Will we go into the great unknown and live with extraterrestrials that can control our minds? All these options are terrifying, almost beyond comprehension. But we must stay calm. We must be kind to each other. Our selfish and cruel behavior got us into this mess. Let's hope changing our ways gets us out," Kate said into the bullhorn. It was so loud many reporters put their hands over their ears. She could see neighbors on their porches listening as well.

"It's honestly all we can do. I have seen the same message in the clouds as you. I have no further information. I wish I knew more, but I don't. Go home. Hug your loved ones. And just wait. It's honestly all we can do," Kate said, entering Sinclair's yard and walking toward his steps. The crowd politely stayed on the sidewalk.

"Good job, Kate," Sinclair said as he opened the front door. "You calmed them down and gave them direction and, I guess, a little hope. Let me get some ice for your lip."

"Welcome home, lovebirds," Jo-Ellen said as soon as the door was open. "Remember these guys?" She pointed to the acting general of Space Force and several other people standing in Sinclair's living room.

Ugh, the last people I want to see! Why did Jo-Ellen let them in?

"Out. Out. Everyone out," Sinclair said, reading Kate's mind. "This is my house and I want you all out now!"

The acting general stood up. "Sorry to barge in on you. We are here by order of the President. We have questions. We need to speak with Rex right now. We must try to shut down whatever he has planned. These two gentlemen are with the Department of Defense. He is from the State Department, and she is from the Speaker's office," he said, pointing to each of his companions in turn.

Kate's fists clenched. *Why don't they get it?* "I can't command Rex to speak to me. He said he would let us know when the others were here and he has! Sure, he used some unnatural extraterrestrial-created cloud that apparently can be seen from everywhere, but he told us. He has enormous power! He does what he wants when he wants. I'm so tired of explaining this to you guys! Just leave!"

Her lip hurt. These people were idiots. She didn't want to waste what precious time remained with them. She wanted to be alone with Sinclair.

"We have to try to reach Rex. You can't give up! Keep trying. People are scared and we have to try and make them safe!" the guy from the Department of Defense insisted.

People are scared? I have tried to calm them and offer them hope. No, he means powerful people in the government are scared and that is what he is worried about! Powerful people look after powerful people; he does not give a shit about regular people.

Sinclair took a step forward. "I presume you don't have a warrant to be in my house—"

Kate rested a hand on his arm to signal she had this. He looked at her and gave a barely perceptible nod. "I understand that you're scared. You're about to lose the little bit of power you've amassed. But, in one way or another, things are about to change. Either many of us are leaving the planet—or we stay here and die. Wouldn't it be great to have a third option, where we all get to stay and improve our planet?

Anyway, we all know and understand the situation and there is nothing left to say. You've overstayed your welcome. Now LEAVE!" Kate shouted.

A cop in full uniform walked out of the kitchen and toward Kate with plastic handcuffs in-hand The others made a path for him to get to Kate.

What the hell? It seems like the few remaining cops in America are always coming at me with handcuffs!

"You can't be serious," Sinclair said, stepping in front of Kate. "This woman has done all she can for us, and you're going to arrest her? Again? She has committed NO crime and you want to make her spend what may be her last hours alive in jail?! No way that is going to happen!"

Kate remembered the bullhorn and brought it to her mouth. "Get out! Get out! Get out!" Everyone jumped, startled by the sudden, extremely loud, and painful words. They all covered their ears and rushed out the front door, including the acting general and the cop with the handcuffs.

Kate kept right on screaming into the bullhorn until they'd all left, even Jo-Ellen.

"Well, that was one sexy way to get me alone," Sinclair laughed, removing his hands from his ears. He took the bullhorn from her hands, setting it down on the couch before pulling her into a hug.

"Geez, I didn't want to be an asshole, but I seriously couldn't take it," Kate said, resting her head against Sinclair's chest. "Sorry if I hurt your ears."

"Knock-knock. I'm back and they're gone," Jo-Ellen said, entering the house.

This woman can't take a hint even if it screamed into her ears with a bullhorn.

Kate sighed and pulled away from Sinclair.

Jo-Ellen patted her on the back. "Smooth move. You blew their last-ditch effort to try and compel Rex to snatch you up. They actually thought that if they held on tight to you, Rex would accidentally take them up too," Jo-Ellen said, shaking her head in disbelief. "That was their plan! I guess they think they can handle Rex better than you. So incredibly stupid."

"Well, ready or not, we're about to find out what the writing in the clouds really means," Kate said, locking eyes with Sinclair.

"Whatever happens, I'm not leaving your side," he promised.

She hoped it was a promise he could keep.

THIRTY-ONE

Sixty-Three Days After the Shooting

After Jo-Ellen mercifully went home, Kate and Sinclair spent the rest of the night talking to friends and family and laughing at shared memories. Sinclair's mom had them cracking up with all the ways she had thought she might die: her terrible driving, being run over by a golf cart, being eaten by an alligator, COVID, or some other dreadful disease. But never did an extraterrestrial skywriter cross her mind. Kate loved her dark humor.

At midnight, Kate and Sinclair walked out into the backyard to look up at the sky and at the eerily bright clouds that still read: "THEY'RE HERE."

She'd never seen such beautiful clouds. It reminded her of the northern lights in Canada, which she had seen once on vacation. She had never gazed upon such a dynamic night sky on the east coast of the United States.

"Yep, and so are we, Rex." Kate laughed. "I don't know why I think everything is so funny. There is nothing funny about this situation."

"We're really tired. And relieved. I mean, we aren't dead yet. We're still here. Might as well make the best of it. Laughing is as good a thing to be doing as anything," Sinclair said, smiling up at the sky.

"I can think of some other good things we can do," Kate said, leaning in to kiss Sinclair's lips, cheek, nose, and neck. She kept giggling until Sinclair kissed her deeply and took her hand, leading her back into the house and up to his bedroom. They fell into bed, laughing.

If this was the moment Rex chose to take them all up, she'd leave Earth on a high note.

THIRTY-TWO

Sixty-Four Days After the Shooting

"**K**ate, wake up!" Sinclair said. He stood at the bedroom window, looking into the bright morning sky.

She could barely open her eyes between the deep sleep he'd interrupted and the bright light. "What?"

"It's gone! I should be able to see it!" Sinclair said.

"Clouds move, right?" Kate sat up and wrapped the sheet around her chest, still a little shy to be naked in front of Sinclair.

"No, it's not a natural cloud. You can't see a real cloud from everywhere. We could definitely see it from here last night. And your mom could see it. Everyone saw it. The whole world saw the same thing. But I think it's gone! Okay, I'm going to check outside to be sure," Sinclair said as he rushed out of the bedroom.

Kate heard him bounding down the stairs, taking two, or three, at a time. She heard him move through the house and open the back door. She swung her legs out of bed and searched the floor for her discarded clothes. As she pulled on some shorts, she heard him calling to her from outside.

"It's really gone, Kate!"

What does this mean? Something good or bad?

Kate went downstairs and out the front door. She wanted to see for herself. She looked up, squinting her eyes, and saw nothing but a blue sky. Not a cloud in sight. As she walked down the steps and the short path that led to the public sidewalk, she found her neighbors idling in the street. One older gentleman started clapping. Others looked at her like she would know why it was gone.

Kate just shrugged and shook her head to let them know she was as clueless as they were.

A police car turned onto the street. Amanda was in the driver's seat.

Kate went back inside Sinclair's house.

She honestly hoped Kyle was finding as much happiness with Amanda as she was with Sinclair.

"Is it gone out front too?" Sinclair asked as he pulled her in for a hug. "I think this is a good sign. I mean, the ominous cloud message is gone and we're still alive! *And* here on Earth!"

Kate kissed him long and slow and smiled, but she had reservations.

Yesterday, we were happy; every second we were alive and on Earth felt precious. Today feels different. I have finally learned not to celebrate too soon. It isn't over yet.

"I'm hungry and dying for some coffee," she managed.

"Sure thing," Sinclair said, heading to the kitchen.

An hour later, they were sitting on the couch watching the news. People around the world were celebrating: dancing in the streets, popping champagne, crying happy tears. Most were wearing masks. Some had signs that read, "Thanks, Rex" or "Hello, Rex." Some people were angry and carried signs that read, "Fuck You, Rex."

Cars honked in celebration. Kate could hear fireworks going off in the distance. This was D.C., and people always had fireworks.

Animals have enough to contend with—pollution, traffic, climate change, habitat loss—why must we add terrifying noise to their difficult lives?

"I'll be curious to see if the President, Congress, and the oil and gas companies stick to their promises now," Sinclair said.

Kate sighed. "I certainly hope so. Not just to stop horrible pollution from killing humans, wildlife, and nature, all of which we need to survive, but also because we don't know what Rex and the others are doing. Seriously, we have no idea what's going on. There could still be more violence."

A call interrupted their conversation. Sinclair accepted the call on his computer with one eager tap.

"Holy shit, if it isn't Adam Cohen, in the virtual flesh," Sinclair said to the screen.

"Hi, Sinclair. How's it going?" Adam asked.

Kate was on the video feed because they had been sitting very close when the call came through. Adam was an older gentleman with grey hair and a grey handlebar mustache. She thought he looked a little like Einstein.

"Okay, I guess. We're alive, on Earth, and I still have a job," Sinclair replied. "At least, I assume I still have a job since I'm still getting direct deposits, not because I have talked to my boss in more than a month."

Kate hadn't even thought about the fact that Sinclair must have been taking time off from work these past few weeks.

"Oh, Kate. Let me introduce you. This is my boss at NASA, Adam Cohen," Sinclair said, nodding toward the computer screen.

"Nice to meet you, Ms. Stellute. You are an American hero. Actually, a planet Earth hero," Adam said with a slightly strange smile. He shifted uncomfortably in his seat.

"Not really. But thanks. And it's nice to meet you, Mr. Cohen. Though I'll leave now—let you guys do your work," Kate said, starting to get up off the couch.

"No wait, Ms. Stellute. Please stay. I'd like to speak with both of you," Adam said.

Sinclair nodded at Kate. "What's up, Adam?" he asked with an angry tone. "It's been a month since I heard from you."

This is intriguing. Sinclair seems pissed off. He never said anything about his job or boss in all the drama of the past several weeks. Not a word. I probably should have asked.

"I know, Sinclair. Your anger is valid. But you know how it is around here. Everything was discombobulated due to the virus and then the shooting sent everything else into chaos. NASA cancelled launches and put holds on everything, and of course, there were power struggles about who was filling roles that had suddenly become available. There were a lot of deaths. No one resigns from NASA. No one retires until they must. Job openings are rare. Things got chaotic," Adam said.

"I honestly don't care about your managerial problems. Launches were still happening," Sinclair said.

"I checked in after I heard about Yvette, remember? You usually work independently so—"

"The past few weeks, when I needed NASA's help, you didn't call me back," Sinclair interrupted. His usually calm voice was filled with tension.

"Okay, hold on. Let me explain. When it first became known you were working with Kate Stellute, and she was a person of interest in the mass shooting, I was told by the higher-ups not to communicate with you," Adam said quickly.

"That's total BS, Adam. We go way back," Sinclair snapped.

"They said you might be in trouble and they didn't want NASA's good name and reputation tarnished by whatever was going on with you and Ms. Stellute. They told me not to engage and that they had everything under control. Then, on September 7, when you were in the control room and we all saw what happened, I started to understand what you had done. I went back to the chain of command and said we needed you back at work. I was told no, again. I was ordered not to communicate with you. This directive was coming from higher than NASA," Adam said, his face flushing red. He took a few deep breaths before continuing.

"In light of everything that has happened, I convinced the higher-ups that you're working to help NASA. Working to help Earth. We need to help you. So, I'm offering Kate a transfer back to NASA from Space Force, to work with us, in our division. We can study the debris more and hopefully understand and explain Rex. She belongs in this division. You know, here, where we discreetly study things from outer space," Adam said.

Kate and Sinclair looked at each other. *A job? At NASA? Doing more than the boring contract work I was saddled with at Space Force?* She couldn't keep the smile off her face

"Huh, interesting. What do you think, Kate?" Sinclair winked. "I'd love to work with you."

What do I think? That this is the opportunity of a lifetime.

Kate channeled all her professionalism. "What are the terms? Is this a real job offer, a detail, or a government transfer that can take months, with me having to constantly ping HR?" Kate asked.

"HR and OPM have been greased and it's all set. You're an 11 at Space Force and can come over here as a 12, and we are offering you a $5,000 bonus. A thank you from NASA for saving the world," Adam said. "You can start tomorrow."

A GS-12? Starting tomorrow. This is awesome, but I will negotiate. My mom told me to never take the first offer. "Interesting. But I would prefer to come in as a GS-14 or 15."

"Ha, I wish, Kate. The 13 is the highest level for a program analyst here and the 14 and 15 are for the management track, which requires special courses you have not taken, or a Ph.D. I wish I could, but I can't change the rules." Adam shrugged.

Kate refrained from rolling her eyes. The government was full of rules to keep people from advancing and to curtail creativity and innovation. The bureaucratic obstacles just made people—especially young people—not want to work for the government. If there were more passionate and creative people working for the federal agencies, perhaps there would have been stronger rules that would have prevented the collision that caused the mass shooting.

"With all due respect, I *am* an expert. I have met with an actual extraterrestrial. I think that trumps a Ph.D. where I'd only research the hypothetical. Go back and say I want a level 15 position and Sinclair needs to get a $5,000 saving the world bonus as well. Oh, and offer Jo-Ellen Marshall a position in your division with the same terms," Kate said, her confidence soaring.

"You drive a hard bargain," Adam answered, trying to hold back a smile. "I'll see what I can do."

Kate smiled from ear to ear. "Okay, do what you can. You know what I want. I mean, I could always write a book, maybe have it made into a movie, and share what I know with the world. I don't need a job at NASA."

"Hold on, Ms. Stellute. On behalf of the government, I'm sure I am authorized to beg you to not do that, at least not yet!" Adam exclaimed.

"Then secure me a GS-15 and everything else I have requested. It was a great pleasure meeting you,

Adam," Kate said, standing and moving away from the camera.

Well, that was fun! And I might have my dream job working with Sinclair!

Kate left the men to finish their call and walked out into the yard. She looked up into the sky. The brilliant blue, cloudless sky.

But then reality hit her again and she shivered.

What is Rex's game? What's going on? Why the big warning? Did Rex convince the others to leave? Will there be more violence?

She silently begged Rex to communicate with her.

Kate jumped when Sinclair came up behind her and put his arms around her.

"The warning is still gone," Sinclair said, squeezing Kate. "And I think it would be really cool if you came to work at NASA. Think of the resources we would have at our disposal. Think of the fun we could have to trying to figure out Rex."

Kate agreed but with sudden reservations. "I don't know. I was so enthralled by NASA for so long. Their work was so inspiring and brilliant and meaningful, but all I think of now is the debris and their habit of treating space as a garbage can. I love it, but it's a callous and selfish agency. Seventy million Americans, hundreds of millions worldwide, and Rex's parents are dead because NASA didn't sound a meaningful alarm or make policy requirements to reduce the danger. We could still be in danger!"

Her heart beat fast as images of the dead after the mass shooting flashed through her mind.

"But you could change it from the inside. Call them out on their bullshit. Make them adhere to the pledge. Go public when they don't," Sinclair said.

"Okay, but I still feel conflicted. I guess if Adam gets me what I want I'll definitely consider it," Kate said. "But, for now, let's celebrate that we are alive and go back to bed."

Kate squealed as Sinclair dramatically grabbed her hands and led her back inside.

"I guess *this* could be our last day on Earth, and I know what I want to spend it doing," Sinclair said, guiding her upstairs.

She couldn't agree more.

THIRTY-THREE

Sixty-Four Days After
the Shooting

Hours later, Kate and Sinclair were awakened by Jo-Ellen knocking on the front door. They quickly dressed and went downstairs to greet her.

"Hey, Jo-Ellen," Kate said. "How are you today?"

"Good. Alive. How are my lovebirds?" Jo-Ellen asked as she sat down on the couch and opened her laptop, not waiting for an answer. "You have several people wanting to speak to you, right now." She quickly checked a few things. "You will want to hear what they have to say."

Kate shook her head and whispered, "No way. I'm disheveled. Not even wearing a bra. No Zoom or camera calls. I'm done with interviews."

Jo-Ellen stood and handed Kate her phone. "You must take this call. It's just a phone call, no camera."

She sighed heavily. "Hello? Kate Stellute speaking."

"Hi? Kate?"

Her stomach hitched.

Is this real?

"Yes, Madam Speaker, this is Kate. How are you?" Kate's eyebrows shot up and she nodded at Jo-Ellen, both surprised and impressed.

"Alive! On Earth!" The Speaker giggled. "I mean, look, the past few days have been very stressful, right?"

"Yes, absolutely. But I need to tell you that it might not be over. I'm happy the cloud warning is gone, but I don't know if the threat is gone. I haven't heard from Rex," Kate said quickly, nervous to be speaking to one of the most powerful people in the world.

"I see," the Speaker said seriously, all laughter gone. "I was hoping for better news."

"I wish I had it, but I don't," Kate said. "The best, most important thing you can do is stay the course. All those great bills that were made into law, to stop global warming and the biodiversity extinction crisis and provide Americans with universal health care and everything else, must stay in place. Please don't walk away from them," Kate pleaded.

"I have no intention of doing so, Kate, none. Do you realize that 200 million Americans have signed your pledge? Not sure what the other 60-some million are thinking, but 200 million is a mandate. The bills have been passed and signed by the President. They will be implemented. Well, as long as there is no more violence," the Speaker said. "I do hope you get to talk to Rex and find out what is going on. I would love to assure the nation that we are safe."

"I wish I could give that assurance to you, to the country, to the world, and to my mom. I really do," Kate said. "And I hope you do more to improve our country. Stop excessive cattle grazing and reform agriculture. We need more organic healthy food and less meat and chemicals. Oh, and reform gun laws so this never happens again. Well, assuming people ever trust guns again. And what about immigration? We need more people in our workforce now, more than ever, right? And we need real racial justice, and the criminal justice system needs to be reformed. There is so much to do!" Kate ticked through the list of things she worried had not been included in the package of bills signed into law.

"D.C. statehood," Sinclair whispered to Kate.

"And D.C. statehood! That would go far in improving our democracy and racial justice, Madame Speaker!" Kate nodded her head enthusiastically at Sinclair.

The Speaker giggled again. "I hear you, Kate, and completely agree! The majority of Americans want these changes. It's the lobbyists and corporate interests that lie and confuse the public. These new laws are a good start, but we are not done. We will reform this nation to be kinder, gentler, and healthier. We are making it happen. Gee, and all it took was a global pandemic, a global mass shooting, and the threat of complete human annihilation to get it done!"

"Yes, thanks to you, good is coming from all this horror and I am grateful for that," Kate said, smiling.

"And I'm grateful for you and your pledge and all you have done. If we are still here in January, and we can do it COVID-safe, you must come to the State of the Union as my guest. I insist. Please let me know if you hear from Rex. I would love a heads up before a broader announcement, if possible," the Speaker said.

Wow, she's such a politician. Making deals in all situations.

"I can't promise anything, but I will consider it," Kate said.

"Excellent! Thank you. Take care, Kate." The Speaker hung up.

"Wow! I was just talking to the Speaker of the House!" Kate said as she gave Jo-Ellen back her phone. "She plans to continue to move forward with a progressive agenda. I hope we live to see it, to see this wonderful new world."

"Me too, Kate," Sinclair said.

"Okay, this one won't be as much fun," Jo-Ellen said, handing Kate her phone again.

"Hello?" Kate said into it.

"Hi, is this Kate Stellute?"

God dammit, Jo-Ellen! I have no desire to speak to the President of the United States.

"Huh, yes, yes, I'm Kate Stellute," Kate said, giving Jo-Ellen an evil eye.

Jo-Ellen just shrugged and whispered, "Civic duty."

"Hi, Kate, I was wondering if you have heard from Rex?" the President asked.

Like she'd tell him if she had. "No, sir."

"Well. We were all under the impression, because you gave us the impression, that we would be dead now, or living on another planet," the President said, sounding annoyed.

"Yes, that's what I was led to believe. I made every-thing I knew clear to the world," Kate said, a little defensively.

"Okay. Right. So, it seems your murderous little friend may also be a liar."

Talk about liars—this guy lies all the time!

"Maybe the circumstances changed for him. I sure hope so," Kate replied stiffly.

"The thing is, Kate, we passed a lot of socialist laws that I was told would complement the pledge, and help Americans look good to Rex. But I fear that when corporate America wakes up, alive and kicking, they won't be happy with these bills that were forced down our throats. We have a huge labor shortage from the pandemic and shooting. We don't need more dramatic changes to our energy and economic sys-tems now. We don't need huge wages or tax increases. That's the last thing America needs. We need stability, to get things back to normal, quickly," the President continued.

Kate cut him off. "Look, Mr. President, I have no idea why we're still alive and still on Earth. I have no idea what *the others* are doing. But if we just start polluting and hurting each other and nature, return to the status quo, business as usual, we might piss them off again."

"Fine, fine, we'll leave space alone," the President said. "But all these other liberal tree-hugging changes are unnecessary. It would be helpful if you were to say something along those lines to Rex, and the media, so we can make some changes—"

Kate cut him off again. "Good luck with that, Mr. President, but I'm not helping you or anyone go back on their word. If we, as a country, have not learned anything meaningful from this crisis, then we deserve what comes." Kate hung up.

"What did the narcissist do?" Jo-Ellen asked.

"Ugh! Nothing yet. I can't stand that guy!" Kate said.

"I guess he has not been briefed on Malcolm's story yet, about the vanishing agents that may have been planning to hurt you," Jo-Ellen said ominously.

Kate looked at Jo-Ellen for a few seconds but did not respond to the comment.

"Don't ever do that again, Jo-Ellen. I never want to speak to that man again," she said.

"Okay. No problem. Just a few more. This is the Post. Do a couple of interviews, they'll spread the word, and you two lovebirds can go back to bed. Okay? Deal?" Jo-Ellen asked, handing her the phone again.

"You are a terrible communications director. You're supposed to prepare me," Kate said taking the phone. "Keep this up, and we won't take you to NASA with us."

"Wait. What?" Jo-Ellen asked.

Kate just smiled at her and said into the phone, "Hi, this is Kate Stellute. With whom am I speaking?"

THIRTY-FOUR

Sixty-Four Days After the Shooting

Sinclair and Kate sat on Sinclair's back porch drinking wine when Jo-Ellen walked out the back door.

"You need to take this call," Jo-Ellen said, handing Kate her phone.

"Nope. I'm done. I told you. It's happy hour and we're being happy," Kate insisted.

"This one is strange. She said she has been making urgent calls all day to track you down. She is desperate to talk to you. I really think you should take it. She is not a political person or the press," Jo-Ellen said. "Just take it."

Kate took the phone with a loud sigh.

"Hello, this is Kate Stellute. With whom am I speaking?"

"Hi, I'm Dr. Samantha Devi with the National Institute of Health," the voice said. "Are you really Kate? Kate Stellute that speaks to Rex?"

"Yes, it's really me. I have communicated through the media everything I know. I have not talked to Rex since the cloud message formed. I don't know what will happen next. Knowing that, what exactly do you want, Dr. Devi?" Kate asked.

"I guess I need advice. When I went into my lab this morning, there was a vial I have not seen before in the refrigerator. There's an orange note on it that reads 'For Kate,'" Dr. Devi said.

A large pit formed in Kate's stomach. She looked at the empty wine bottles, the joyous and relaxed look on Sinclair's face.

Maybe we celebrated too soon.

"What's in the vial?" Kate asked. She closed her eyes, dreading the response.

"I have no idea. I have not opened it. I'm worried that it's from Rex or the others and I imagine you understand why I would not open it," Dr. Devi said, sounding distressed at her own words.

"Well, maybe it's a joke? A bad joke or maybe a hoax? Did you ask your colleagues? Anyone there named Kate?" Kate asked, slightly joking, trying to lighten the mood.

"No one that works here is called Kate. I know everyone with access to this floor. I know everyone that works in this building. Very few people work here, and no one is named Kate. And yes, I asked everyone with access to this room if they put it in the refrigerator with the note. They all said no," Dr. Devi said.

"How many people have access? What do you mean by very few?" Kate asked, still hopeful it was a bad joke.

Or better yet, this has nothing to do with me. Who is this woman? What kind of lab? How well does this doctor know her colleagues? This all sounds fishy. And a little scary.

"Eight people currently have access to this floor, and I have spoken with all of them. I believe they do not know how it got here and are as concerned as I am," Dr. Devi replied.

Kate squeezed her eyes shut. *Only eight people at an NIH lab? In a pandemic? That doesn't make sense.*

"Kate, would you please come here and help us figure this out? Maybe you will see something that will make us better understand the situation. We would really appreciate it," Dr. Devi said.

"Okay. Sure. I will come," Kate said. She opened her eyes and saw concern in Sinclair's and Jo-Ellen's. "I know where NIH is located. I will come in the morning. I will text you when we are close."

"We are not at NIH headquarters in the beltway. We are at a lab in Maryland. I will send the address. And we really want you to come tonight. Right now, if you can. We would really, really appreciate it," Dr. Devi insisted.

An anxious wave of nausea rushed through Kate. She glanced over at her almost empty wine glass.

How many glasses have I had? What am I committing to? Why does this seem so ominous? I don't want to go.

"Okay, sure. We will leave shortly and get there when we get there, I guess," Kate winced as she spoke, her words contradicting her thoughts.

Sinclair lifted his eyebrows, and mouthed *What?*

"Wonderful! Thank you so much! See you soon!" Dr. Devi hung up.

"What's going on, Kate?" Sinclair asked.

"I'm not sure, but we are heading to a NIH lab in Maryland. The staff found a vial with my name on it," Kate said. "And I have a bad feeling about it."

THIRTY-FIVE

Sixty-Four Days After
the Shooting

A s Jo-Ellen drove, Kate fiddled with the radio to distract herself, pausing when a song or an interview caught her attention. She was mentioned in almost every story with recordings of her answers during previous interviews being played over and over. When she heard her own voice, she would twist the knob to find the next station.

"I have been trying to reach Kate Stellute all day," a woman who sounded a little like the NIH doctor said. Kate paused to listen.

"We are big political donors and have begged elected officials to get us to her, but we have been rebuffed," the woman said.

Okay, that's definitely not the NIH doctor.

Kate reached for the button to move on but Jo-Ellen stopped her. "This sounds interesting. Can we listen for a second?"

Kate just shrugged and turned it up.

"I really want to thank her. I am a leader in my religion and we send mind-files into space for some members of our congregation. It ensures their essence, their memories, and their existence, continue when their body fails. It's a very expensive process and the mind-files are precious. When Kate cleaned up the debris and made space safe, she also helped preserve the mind-files. We had no idea how dangerous the situation had become in space. We are forever grateful and I am eager to speak with Kate directly. Perhaps also communicate with Rex…"

Kate, Sinclair, and Jo-Ellen all burst out laughing, missing whatever the person said next.

"Huh, maybe when we pulverized the debris, we also pulverized the mind-files. I wonder if she thought of that?" Sinclair asked, and they all laughed some more.

"Kate, this could be a business opportunity! I bet you could make a lot of money; the woman said the process was expensive. If you assure her congregation the mind-files are safe and sound and that they should continue to zap them into space, well, you should be paid for your knowledge and expertise," Jo-Ellen added, and they all laughed again.

The chitchat and laughter made Kate feel better. But as she continued to scroll through the radio stations, she only paused for music. She hoped that woman wasn't a charlatan taking advantage of her congregation. She did not want to hear any lies or scary news that would make her more worried. The mysterious vial was enough.

"Do you think Space Force, NASA, and DOD know we are on our way to this lab?" Kate asked.

"I did not tell them, but I'm sure we are being monitored, especially you, Kate. They probably know your every move. And I think they will for a long time," Jo-Ellen said.

"It'll be interesting to see who is at the lab. Maybe they will beat us there," Sinclair added.

"It would be nice if they sorted it out before we got there and were actually helpful for a change," Kate said.

THIRTY-SIX

Sixty-Four Days After the Shooting

An hour later, Jo-Ellen pulled into the large empty parking lot of a plain cement office building. It had eight floors and a business name Kate had never heard of on a large neon sign.

"Well, Space Force and the others aren't here," Jo-Ellen said.

"This does not look like a lab," Sinclair said. "Is this the correct address?"

"Yep. I think so. I mean, this is the address she texted. It doesn't say NIH anywhere obvious. Looks like an insurance building or call center," Jo-Ellen said.

Two guards walked out of the lobby toward the car. They were in full protective gear and plastic face-guards. Neither had a gun.

"Hi. Kate Stellute?" One peered into the driver's window, looking past Jo-Ellen. "There you are. I recognize you from the news. And Dr. Sinclair Jones." He nodded toward Sinclair in the back seat. "The docs are expecting you. They're eager for you to go downstairs."

As they were escorted into the lobby, Jo-Ellen asked, "Is this a lab? An NIH lab?"

"Yes. The doctors will explain everything. Please just follow us into this room and put on this protective gear." One of the guards held a door open for them.

"What the hell? That is level ten COVID, Ebola, contagion-type gear!" Jo-Ellen exclaimed, looking at the elaborate outfits.

"Seriously! How do you even put that on?" Kate asked. It looked like a scary space suit to her.

"We will show you. And if you want to go down, you have to put it on. You can stay here if you like, Ms. Marshall. They are only expecting Ms. Stellute and Dr. Jones," one of the guards said, looking at Jo-Ellen.

"I'm going," Jo-Ellen said with a sigh. "I drove all the way here. I want to see what the fuss is about."

It took several minutes for them to put on the extensive protective gear. When they were dressed, the guards led them to an elevator.

"Ebola, COVID, SARS, MERS—they all came from exploiting wildlife. When animals are tortured and abused while being captured, caged, moved, or in slaughterhouses and markets, their immune systems weaken, and they can get sick. Their viruses can jump between animals and humans, creating deadly diseases and pandemics. Did you know that?" Jo-Ellen asked.

"Yes," everyone responded at the same time, including the guards.

"Well, they were not created in a lab," Jo-Ellen chattered nervously.

"We know," everyone said.

They entered the elevator and went down several floors.

"How far down are we going?" Kate asked.

"Far. All the way to the basement. You are going to the most important lab and its way down. In fact, we can't exit this elevator. When we get down to the bottom, different guards will escort you to Dr. Devi," a guard answered.

"Jesus," Jo-Ellen breathed. "Maybe Rex is down there and wants to grab us and sneak us off to space."

"He would not need to sneak us up. He can take us from anywhere, even this scary elevator. Just snatch us up," Kate said with a dramatic flick of her wrist.

"And the docs better not hurt us. Remember what happened to Malcolm's agents?" Jo-Ellen added.

The two guards looked at each other with large, fearful eyes.

The elevator finally stopped and opened. Two guards were waiting in the hall, as promised.

"Ms. Stellute, Dr. Jones, Ms. Marshall, please follow us," a guard said. He was in full protective gear as well. "You will go in here and add this additional layer to your gear."

"Jesus!" Jo-Ellen said again when she saw the next layer: a breathing apparatus connected to an oxygen tube.

"This is like a space suit. Seriously, just like a space suit," Sinclair said, looking at the contraption. "Even has little microphones so we can hear each other talk. This is intense. Where are we? What is down here? What is NIH working on? Maybe this is a mistake,

Kate. Maybe they want to run tests on you. Maybe we should leave!"

"No wonder the government goons from Space Force and DOD aren't here because this is scary," Jo-Ellen said. "Let Kate take care of the dangerous stuff!"

"This is just too strange. This whole thing is bizarre. But I need to find out why my name is on that note," Kate said calmly, trying to reassure Sinclair and Jo-Ellen.

"We don't know if you are the Kate in the note. It didn't have your last name," Sinclair said, still sounding worried, as they connected his suit to the tube.

Once they were fully dressed and had checked to be sure they could all hear one another, they were led down a long, dark hall. The walls seemed to be made of cement and steel.

As they walked slowly and awkwardly down the hall, Kate said, "You might be right, Sinclair. This is really creepy. I have seen this hallway in a dozen movies. It's always incredibly scary and generally does not end well for the characters."

"Says the woman that has been in the white room with an extraterrestrial," Jo-Ellen said.

When they reached the end of the hall, the guard started to open a huge door. Instead of a doorknob or keypad, he used a huge, circular contraption.

"Jesus Christ! That looks like a hatch in a submarine. Where the hell are we? Are we underwater?" Jo-Ellen asked, her voice rising with fear.

Just then the lock gave and the door opened. Standing inside were three people in similar gear.

"Hi, Kate, I mean Ms. Stellute! Welcome to our lab! Thank you for coming. And you as well, Dr. Jones and Ms. Marshall, of course. I'm Dr. Devi and these are my colleagues, Dr. Rubin and Dr. Richards. If you would follow us through here, that would be great."

They entered a brightly lit room that looked like a regular lab to Kate. Not creepy or scary. She took a deep breath and tried to relax.

"Okay, this seems more normal. What's with all the protective gear and exactly how close are we to the molten lava layer?" Jo-Ellen asked.

"Ha, not nearly deep enough for lava," Dr. Devi responded. "We have a few very dangerous and deadly chemicals and viruses here so we have to be extremely careful. And this lab is top secret. Under normal conditions, you would never be allowed down here or even know it exists."

"Let me guess: you have coronavirus down here?" Jo-Ellen asked.

"I don't want to know. Honestly, I'm sick of secrets and lies and greed and activities that hurt people. Just show me the note and the vial," Kate said.

"Kate, we do good work here. Our research saves lives. Honestly," Dr. Devi said. "Please, follow me."

If I see an animal being experimented on, I will lose my shit. Maybe I should cover my eyes.

"It's so clean. Do you actually do work here? Real research?" Sinclair asked.

"We only have a few employees here at a time because of the pandemic. But even before, very few people worked here so it's easy, and good practice, to keep it clean and sterile. Oh, here we are. This is my lab and my refrigerator," Dr. Devi said as she entered a little room. "You can see through the glass doors that there is the vial right there, with the orange note." She pointed at it. "You can clearly read the words, 'For Kate.'"

Everyone peered at the vial and the note.

"Seems very anti-climactic. Should we open it and let Kate have a closer look?" Jo-Ellen asked.

"No!" Dr. Devi and the other scientists cried at the same time.

"I was kidding," Jo-Ellen muttered. "Just trying to lighten the mood."

"What do you think it is?" Sinclair asked.

"We have no idea. As you have seen, we have very strict security here. No one gets in here that is not allowed. We have cameras everywhere watching us and our work. We are so concerned about this vial; we only told a few other NIH staff. Everyone is sworn to secrecy because if it gets out, then this lab will be exposed. But it appears someone got in here and left this vial, and note, for Kate," Dr. Devi said. "We have no idea how or why."

Kate stared at the note.

"As I said before, we considered if it could be a bad joke or hoax from a staff member. We watched all the footage between the last time I looked in this refrigerator and the time the note appeared. No one entered this lab. Not one person. And before you suggest a ghost, like one of our guards did, we considered that and rejected it. With all the attention on Rex and Kate, we decided it was best to risk exposure of this top-secret lab's very existence and invite Kate here," Dr. Devi explained.

"Rex has never written me a personal note. The handwriting does not look like the cloud message. Do you recognize the handwriting?" Kate asked.

"No. It doesn't match any of ours," Dr. Devi said.

"What about the vial? Is it one of yours?" Kate asked.

"No. It doesn't look like any we use in this lab. It's a little unusual, but it could be used elsewhere. Maybe at other U.S. government labs? We don't know for sure. We just know it's not used here." Dr. Devi shrugged.

"Maybe it's from space. Like the tech at Kennedy," Jo-Ellen suggested

Why do these bizarre things keep happening to me? But I have come this far. I might as well see it through.

"Okay. Here is what we are going to do. You all are going to leave this room. Go far. Up that elevator and back to the lobby. Go somewhere safe and I'll open it and see if it kills me," Kate said.

"Very funny, Kate," Sinclair said, trying to put a protective arm around her but failing with all the bulky gear they were wearing.

"I'm totally serious, Sinclair. Think about it. Rex and the others can kill us with their minds. They can make us kill ourselves. Maybe this is the violence. Maybe they want it to blend in with the pandemic. I don't know. Maybe, like the shooting, they want it to be fast? But that seems like a Rex thing. Maybe the others are forcing Rex to do something. Maybe whatever is in that vial will kill us slowly, with more pain.

We don't know what the others want. But we have to find out. What else can we do?" Kate asked.

Will it hurt?

"Just leave it there! Just leave it sitting in the refrigerator. Seal off this lab and just leave it," Sinclair said.

"For how long? For some unsuspecting person, years from now, to stumble across it and open it?" Kate asked.

"Sure, why not. At least we would have a few years, maybe a long time before anyone finds it and opens it. And it could kill you, Kate," Sinclair said. "No way you are opening that vial. No way in hell!"

Kate didn't want to die this way. But she had to see this thing through. "Sinclair, the note says it's for me. If I open it and it kills me, keep this room, this lab, sealed off. Keep the public safe if you can. Let's be happy it was left here. Maybe that's Rex's plan? Maybe he told the others to leave a deadly, who-knows-what on Earth, and then he put it in a secure lab with my name on it. He knew I would come and take care of it. Another clever loophole," Kate said, staring at the vial.

"No way in hell, Kate! No way I'm leaving and no way you are opening it!" Sinclair exclaimed. He turned Kate away from the refrigerator, taking her gloved hand in his huge protective glove.

"Okay, this is becoming a lovebird squabble. How far back do we need to go to be safe?" Jo-Ellen asked Dr. Devi. "I mean, I need to be safe to record what happens and share it with the world when the time is right. I'm Kate's communications director. If they die, the world needs to know. If they die and it can spread and take out the world, the world needs to know that too," Jo-Ellen said.

The butterflies in Kate's stomach were as big as crows, but she didn't want Sinclair to know how scared she was.

"Oh, okay. I guess that makes sense. We need to go back up. Let's seal Kate off at several spots. There are cameras everywhere so we will be able to see and hear what happens," Dr. Devi said. "Though I certainly hope no one dies."

"No way. This is not happening," Sinclair said, clearly upset.

"Sinclair, we've all been living under a cloud of doom, literally. We've been living in a world of illness, death, and heartbreak since the pandemic started. In a terrifying and violent world since July 14. We are all in a state of trauma. You and I more than anyone. We are all scared, but we need to move forward. We need to know what is in that vial. Whatever happens, happens," Kate said, as she moved in to give Sinclair a very awkward hug.

They couldn't get close enough to each other, so instead, she touched her gloved hand to the glass screen covering his face.

"Please, Sinclair, I want you to go to a safe place with them," Kate said.

"No way that is going to happen. Jo-Ellen's right. She kept saying 'if they die.' We've been in this together since the beginning. We are each other's lucky charm. You guys go. I'm staying with Kate," he said.

"Okay. I totally knew that was how this would go down," Jo-Ellen said as she walked out of the room.

"Don't do anything until we are out and you hear from us. It will take us several minutes to get up to a safe level," Dr. Devi said as she walked out.

The other two scientists quickly followed Jo-Ellen and Dr. Devi. Kate could hear doors being slammed shut and locked as they headed back to the elevator.

"I don't recall any other solid doors except that first huge submarine-style one on the way in, did you?" Sinclair asked.

"Nope. We are definitely being locked in here," Kate said, nerves firing through her entire body.

Are we being set up?

THIRTY-SEVEN

Sixty-Four Days After the Shooting

"Okay, let's think this through. It could be a trap. Rex's colleagues, the others, lured you in here knowing you would open it and spread some terrible disease all over the world," Sinclair said, pacing.

"Yes, that is definitely one option, Admiral Ackbar. There are many unknown variables. The others could be hurting Rex, me, and everyone because the option of Rex pulling us up before the others destroy humanity might be gone. Rex might have missed the window to save us. Maybe the others are angry Rex even wanted to? Rex might think we are safe. Maybe he left and the others doubled back and created this trap," Kate speculated.

They both stared at the vial in silence

"Another option is that I open it and Dr. Jones watches my face melt off," Kate said, trying not to laugh, but failing.

The world might come to an end. I might die. But I feel oddly giddy. Maybe it's nerves. Maybe it's adrenalin. Maybe it's love.

Sinclair chuckled.

"Okay, lovebirds, not sure why any of this is funny, but I think it's time to get serious." Jo-Ellen's voice came booming over a sound system. "Can we lower the volume for Christ's sake? I sound like Kate with a bullhorn."

"Kate, the gloves will make you very clumsy. Why don't you try picking up a couple of things first, to get a feel for it?" Dr. Devi asked with a much lower volume.

"Okay. Good suggestion. Can you see us clearly?" Kate asked into her microphone. She could hear the question repeat through the intercom.

"Yes, we can see and hear you clearly," Jo-Ellen said. "Please be careful."

Kate went to a table and picked up an empty test tube out of a rack. It slipped through her gloved fingers, hitting the table and smashing into pieces.

"Whoops!" Kate said, laughing. "Look at all that debris!"

"Try two hands, Kate," Sinclair suggested.

Kate pulled another tube out with one hand and placed it in her other hand to prevent it from slipping. She moved it to another table and gently put it down.

"Ta-da!" she said with a flourish. "I think I'm ready. I will take it out with two hands, place it here, and try to open it."

As Kate went to open the refrigerator door, Sinclair stopped her.

"We might die, and I want to say—" Sinclair started.

"I think we said all we needed to on that picnic table, Sinclair," Kate said, smiling at him. "I love you. And I hope every little thing is gonna be alright."

"Well, I hope like crazy we don't die. And I love you too," Sinclair said.

Kate gasped as her heart did happy flips.

"Don't make her cry! Kate cries way too easily! It will fog her headgear and blur her vision, and she will drop the damn vial!" Jo-Ellen said loudly. "Please focus, Kate. It's time to do what you do. Be brave."

Oh my God! In all the rush and panic, I forgot what Rex had said, the story he had told me.

"What's wrong, Kate?" Sinclair demanded, seeing the look of pure panic cross her face.

"It's something Rex said in the white room. Jo-Ellen just reminded me. Rex said he was watching Earth, trying to figure out why we are so self-destructive. He was going to kill every living thing on the planet, but then he realized how wonderful life on Earth really is. He liked nature and animals and all the vibrant energy. So, he decided to just kill the humans because he figured out that humans caused the pollution and debris that destroyed his parent's ship and killed them," Kate said.

Sinclair nodded, encouraging her to go on.

"Rex said he studied the humans and found the ones that go into space. He studied the people at NASA and Space Force because he found us to be the most dominant in space. He went deeper to see why we were so hell-bent on killing ourselves, so he studied individuals. Somehow, he found me. He became intrigued by my contradictions, being a kind loving person, while working for an organization that was so selfish and destructive. He changed into people I admire and respect: Jane Goodall and Jane Fonda, and others. He said I taught him there were good, caring people that tried to stop pollution. He learned that Earth had good people as well as bad. He said I made him decide to not kill everyone," Kate explained quickly, becoming more anxious with each word.

She paused, a chill running down her spine because of what she was about to say.

"It's okay. Go on, Kate," Sinclair encouraged.

"Rex said he asked himself, what would Kate do? Who would Kate punish? And he morphed into Theo Mast with his big scary gun. Rex said, for all my beautiful and kind energy, many humans have dark, cruel, fearful, and angry energy. He said the one common denominator of those people that are driven by hate and fear was guns. He said when he made the connection, the solution was so simple. It only took a few minutes," Kate said.

No one said a word.

"Sinclair, without knowing it, I chose the punishment. I helped kill all those people on July 14. Maybe I'm here to do it again," Kate said, looking at the vial.

"Jesus Christ, Kate! You only thought to tell us now? What did I say that triggered this incredible memory of this terrifying story—that you forgot to tell anyone about until now?" Jo-Ellen shrieked.

"Rex thought I was brave to confront Theo Mast. He picked me as the messenger because he thought I was brave," Kate replied. "Remember when you called me brave, Jo-Ellen, that night in the Space Force conference room? You said you did not know why the word 'brave' was on the list."

"I had no idea! I did not know about Theo Mast or his gun. I did an internet search on you, but it didn't come up. I watched your house for hours and was bored. Pretty basic agent shit. Like I told you before, I was handed a list before the interview that someone downloaded from your computer. I had no idea Rex actually called you brave or why it was on a list!" Jo-Ellen said, her voice still high with nervous anger.

"You are very brave, Kate. Rex was right about that. You are the bravest person I know," Sinclair said, reaching his hand up like he wanted to stroke her face.

She wished she could feel his touch one more time, especially if this was the end.

"Maybe your past helped him choose the punishment, but you also helped him choose who to spare. You helped him clean up space and made it safe for the rest of us. You are brave," Sinclair said.

"But what if I have chosen the new way to kill us? What if it's this?" Kate asked, pointing at the vial with the note.

"Okay, we know you hate guns. What else do you hate?" Jo-Ellen asked.

"Lots of things: some hunters, cruelty, pollution, greed, liars, pandemics. So many things!" Kate said, her voice going up with each thing she listed.

"And that was all in the pledge, Kate. Everything you hate is out in the open. I don't think you are causing this, whatever this is," Sinclair said, nodding at the refrigerator with the vial. "We don't even know for sure this is from Rex or the others."

"Why am I thinking of a large marshmallow man?" Jo-Ellen asked.

Kate rolled her eyes and laughed. Sinclair and Jo-Ellen did as well. They laughed hard for a couple of minutes.

"Hi, so this is Dr. Devi. I'm not sure what is happening or what is so funny. I'm really confused. This is very scary to me and my colleagues. Do you think we should open the vial?"

Kate looked at Sinclair and gave a small nod.

THIRTY-EIGHT

Sixty-Four Days After the Shooting

Kate took several deep breaths and walked over to the refrigerator, pulling the door open. She slowly and gently picked up the vial with the orange note with one gloved hand and placed her other hand under it. She very carefully put the vial in a rack on the table. She carefully removed the note and put it on the table. She gave Sinclair one last long look. He smiled at her and nodded encouragingly.

"We are here for you both. You are heroes to the world. As your communications director, I will make sure, if I survive this and you don't, that the world knows what you did. What you sacrificed," Jo-Ellen said.

Kate slowly unscrewed the top of the vial. It was hard to grip and took longer than it would without the big gloves. Finally, she lifted the top and placed it on the table, near the vial. She then leaned down and put her fully geared head next to it, inhaling deeply.

Nothing happened.

A few seconds later, she straightened and smiled at Sinclair.

They stared at each other for another full minute, waiting.

"This will not teach us anything," Kate said, pulling off her gloves and then her helmet and face shield, unplugging from the oxygen tube as she did so.

"Wait, Kate, no!" shouted Dr. Devi. "You should go in slow steps!"

"Oh, well, too late now," Kate said. She leaned down over the vial and inhaled again.

Sinclair struggled to get his equipment off.

"Well, it has not melted my face or caused immediate death," Kate said, still leaning over the vial.

"Let's try my face," Sinclair said, as he leaned over the vial and inhaled deeply. "Doesn't have any smell that I can detect."

"Jesus," Jo-Ellen said, exhaling a long, loud breath. "They're alive! Alive!"

"Come here," Sinclair said, pulling Kate in for a hug and long kiss.

"Okay, we are thrilled there was no immediate impact, but that is a secure lab, and you are contaminating it. I don't think it's a healthy place for kissing under any circumstances," Dr. Devi remarked over the intercom.

When they pulled out of the embrace, Kate was laughing again.

"Okay, sorry we are messing up your safe space here. So, what is next?" Kate asked. She leaned down to the open vial again and with her face very close asked, "Should I just lick it?"

"No!" Jo-Ellen, Dr. Devi, and Sinclair all shouted at once, making Kate jump, startled by their intense and loud reaction.

"No, that is totally unnecessary, Kate! Now that we know it does not cause airborne immediate death, we can come in with all our proper gear, and run tests," Dr. Devi said. "We will still treat it like Ebola, smallpox, and coronavirus combined. We know how to work with these deadly strains. We needed you to see if it was some otherworldly chemical that killed on impact. It appears not to be, thank God."

"Okay, that's cool," Kate said.

"But since you took your gear off, we hope you will stay a few days, and see if it manifests into an illness. And, even after you leave, you will have to quarantine for three weeks, to be safe," Dr. Devi said.

"Now they tell us! A few days, here! I fear there will be more than kissing contaminating this lab," Kate said, winking at Sinclair.

"It's so strange. Why would Rex or the others do this, if they did? Just to cause more trauma? A slower, scarier, and more painful death? Or is it a sick joke? Maybe one of the scientists did put the note there. I mean, there are plenty of people that still blame you for the death of their loved ones in the shooting," Sinclair pointed out.

"I don't know. But what I do know is we have many days to think about it and discuss it since we are stuck here. And, who knows? Maybe the liquid in that vial will kill the world. Maybe we have become the vectors that will destroy humankind. Maybe we will cause the violence," Kate said, a chill running down her spine.

EPILOGUE

Ninety-Two Days After the Shooting

"**G**ood news," Kate said looking at her phone. "We are negative for everything, including COVID-19. Scrolling, scrolling, scrolling and I still don't know what many of these tests are, but we are negative for everything. Sometimes I think the whole thing was a hoax. There was nothing in that vial."

"So that is that. We were clear last week, but this is a nice cherry on top. I'm less worried about seeing people in person with those results," Sinclair said, not taking his eyes off the road. "Kind of crazy we have not gotten COVID through this whole ordeal."

"Seriously, of course, we are heading to Florida, the COVID capital of America. But whatever, I can't wait to get there!" Kate said, watching green fields and woods fly by as they drove down I-95. "I can't wait to swim in the ocean and run on the beach and see Karisma and hug my mom!"

"Just six hours to go," Sinclair said, smiling. "I am also very eager to get there. I'm not even worried about Florida racists anymore."

Kate hadn't felt so good since before the pandemic. "I feel free! Just flying down this still jarringly empty highway, I feel completely free!" She put her hands in the air and yelled "Yee-haw" in her best southern drawl.

After several days in that lab and twenty-one days in Sinclair's house, she could not be happier to be out. She loved Sinclair with all her heart, but those last few days were trying. They started sneaking out in the middle of the night for runs in the park when they knew they would not see another human. They had to get out to maintain their sanity. Though making love day and night was fun; it was like they were on an extended honeymoon.

Kate took Sinclair's hand and squeezed it.

"I can't wait to take midnight swims with you. I've never had a pool, have you?" Sinclair asked.

"Nope," Kate answered. The pool in their rental would be great, but she couldn't wait to swim in the ocean.

"Since we are both expert-level staff at NASA now, we'll have free range in the hangar to study the collision debris," Sinclair said, as excited as a kid on Christmas. "We're supposed to meet Jack and Jo-Ellen at the hangar next week and get right to work. Well, after lots of swimming."

Kate winked at him. "And some other activities."

"I'm happy NASA hired Jo-Ellen. Though it's strange she still wants to be our communications director. I mean, she deserves whatever she wants. Providing groceries and other necessities for weeks must have been a huge drag, despite her saying it wasn't. I hope she is having some fun before we get to work," Kate said.

"I think Jo-Ellen is fine. I think she knows how lucky we have all been throughout this crazy experience, and she is a natural communications director," Sinclair said.

Kate got lost in her thoughts, remembering some of the fun they had in the lab and in quarantine, most of it in bed.

"Jo-Ellen's media rollout about us being heroes and saving the world, once we cleared quarantine, was a little over the top. It was clever of her to let the world believe we had COVID. But letting the world believe we somehow made the ominous cloud disappear was definitely not true. We don't know what happened to the cloud. We just cleared the debris," Sinclair added. "Oh well, I think she loves scheduling interviews as much as she loved tracking space debris."

"The worst was all those people asking me over and over: 'Are we safe? Is it over? Did the pledge work? Are the others gone? What is Rex thinking? Will there be more violence?' And having to say over and over and over, 'I don't know. I know nothing. I have not talked to Rex and I have no idea if we are safe.' That was unpleasant. I felt so useless," Kate said, looking up at the sky.

"We may never know whether the pledge worked or if we're still in mortal danger. We need to accept that we live in an uncertain world. We are never going to be entirely safe. We are not in control. We all need to live for the moment and love each other and life. It's all we can do," Sinclair said.

"Well, we may not be in control, but we can do things to make our world better and safer for everyone and everything in it. I'm sure as hell going to use my celebrity to keep Congress and the President true to the pledge and the laws they passed," Kate said.

Sinclair's phone rang. "It's Harriet. It's strange that she would call me on the phone, I mean, she is a teenager."

"Hi, Uncle Sinclair! May I speak to Kate? It's very important," Harriet said.

"Of course, she's right here. You're on speaker."

"Hi, Harriet. What's up? Everything okay?" Kate asked.

"No. I heard something shocking at school," Harriet said, without any small talk. "Turns out that rich cattle space guy donated $1,000,000 to a big national environmental organization."

Kate smiled. Charitable giving was still skyrocketing. Even if it could be performative, she'd take it. "What's wrong with that?"

"Well, the organization *said* it was going to use it to address the climate crisis. They *said* they were planning to use the money to put a satellite into space to track where global warming gasses are being emitted, which is totally stupid and wasteful because we already know where they are coming from. Cars! Cows! Power plants! Manufacturing! And this group is paying the rich space guy to take the satellite up, so he gets part of his donation back! Can you believe that? They should use the money to put solar panels on roofs!" Harriet exclaimed, outraged.

Kate loved that Sinclair's niece was so environmentally conscious. She hoped the rest of the mass shooting survivors felt the same. Everyone would be vital in holding Congress's feet to the fire. As well as holding one another accountable through their personal choices. "That totally sucks. I agree, it's bullshit," Kate responded.

"Each launch emits around 1000 tons of carbon dioxide! So, the environmental organization is actually using the donation to contribute to global warming. And they are taking the cash from the cattle king so the money was made by causing global warming. Raising and eating cattle causes global warming. Shooting rockets into space causes global warming. It's so hypocritical! And it's killing our planet and us! Like, watch us create the first category 6 hurricane!" Harriet was fuming.

"Yes, it's terrible. I'm so happy you made this connection. We need to bring this bullshit out into the light. I don't think most Americans are capable of making the connections, which allows the cattle king to pollute and kill and make billions. Not sure what's up with that particular environmental organization. Looks like the conservation sector needs to clean up its act, just like the space industry. We still have a lot of work to do," Kate said. She knew it would take time to undo all the harmful patterns of the past.

"Anyway, I needed to vent to someone who would understand. I'm so angry, but talking to you helps," Harriet said, sounding calmer.

"Keep talking to everyone. People have to change their ways. Every one of our choices has consequences," Kate said.

"And I'm confused. If they signed the pledge, don't they have to stop polluting and eating meat?" Harriet asked.

"The pledge is not a legally binding document. Technically, people pledged to change their behavior in order to get to go into space with Rex, or really, they agreed to adhere to the pledge *in space*. We have to remind people that Rex and the others could come back. But ideally, as people live in more healthy and kinder ways, they and the natural world around them will thrive and they won't need the pledge as a reason to do so," Kate said.

She'd double-check which environmentalists had signed the pledge later and be sure to remind them of their commitments.

"Thanks, Kate. I have so many other things to share when you get down here. Drive safe, Uncle Sinclair!" Harriet said before she hung up.

"Okay, this is something we can do right away at NASA: require they paint their global warming gas emissions on every rocket, so the world sees the damage," Kate said, sighing. "They can take the consequences into consideration when deciding if a launch is really worth it."

"And what about ozone depletion and damage to the stratosphere? That's extremely dangerous too," Sinclair noted.

She loved that her fight was now his too. She loved that she did not have to convince him these concerns were valid.

"We have so much work to do. It's overwhelming. But we can't give up. We must make everyone that signed the pledge adhere to its goals," Kate said. "We must never reignite the others' wrath again."

"I have complete faith you will, Kate. We got really lucky because of you, and the world needs to remember that." Sinclair took her hand and kissed it.

I got lucky finding love during so much pain and terror.

"And they never did find those two guys claiming to be agents. If Malcolm's story ever got out, it might prevent people from trying to finesse the pledge or backslide on their commitments," Kate replied, glancing up at the sky.

She shook her head, trying to block out dark thoughts on such a beautiful day, but they came anyway.

It still made her a little sad to think about Kyle. She had watched from Sinclair's front window as he and Amanda packed up a small moving truck. He moved in with Amanda. It was all for the best, but Kate cried watching him load the truck. She and Kyle had so many great times together and had really loved each other before the mass shooting changed everything.

Kate's phone buzzed in her lap. Sinclair peered over to see who it was. "Is that Jackie? Eager for our ETA?" Sinclair asked.

Kate stared at her phone, speechless. "Not Mom, breaking news from the Washington Post, NPR, CNN, FOX, NEWSY…"

"Well, what is it?" Sinclair asked. "The last big breaking news was when we were released from quarantine. What is it now, Kate? Is it bad?"

"A pharmaceutical company announced it has created a vaccine for COVID-19. Preliminary testing has gone extremely well. They are looking for thousands of volunteers to continue tests," Kate said, reading the announcement. "Government officials said it's miraculous and will be the fastest vaccine ever created. It could save millions of lives."

"Wow, that's fantastic news!" Sinclair said, kissing Kate's hand again. "Thank God!"

Kate got goosebumps everywhere.

What was in that vial?

Did the vial contain the vaccine?

"No, not God. I think we need to thank Rex," Kate said, looking skyward.

THE END

QUESTIONS AND TOPICS
FOR DISCUSSION

1. Kate and Sinclair debate over a moral dilemma. What is that dilemma and whose side would you take? Why?

2. Kate takes solitude, strength, and pleasure in nature. What activities bring you peace and/or make you feel you are living life to the fullest?

3. People often judge themselves by their intentions but judge others by their actions. Can you name a few examples of this from the story? From your life?

4. Were you surprised by the evolution of Kate and Kyle's relationship? How about Kate and Sinclair's? How did the changes make you feel?

5. Do you think people are capable of real, meaningful change? Why or why not?

6. The Impact Series discusses many forms of pollution. Can you name a few? Do you think

any are more dangerous than others? If so, which ones and why?

7. What characters do you like most and least in *The Judgment*? Why?

8. Do you think there was an abuse of power in the story? If so, by whom and do you think it was justified?

9. What harsh truths do you prefer to ignore? What harsh truths does the government ignore?

10. Kate interacts with many women in this story. What do these women teach her? What elements within the range of feminism do they represent, such as political, economic, personal, and social equity of the sexes? How about in relation to gun violence?

11. Is it possible to live a normal life and not ever tell a lie? How about not hurting others and treating everyone and everything with respect and kindness? Is it possible?

12. Would you sign the pledge? Why or why not?

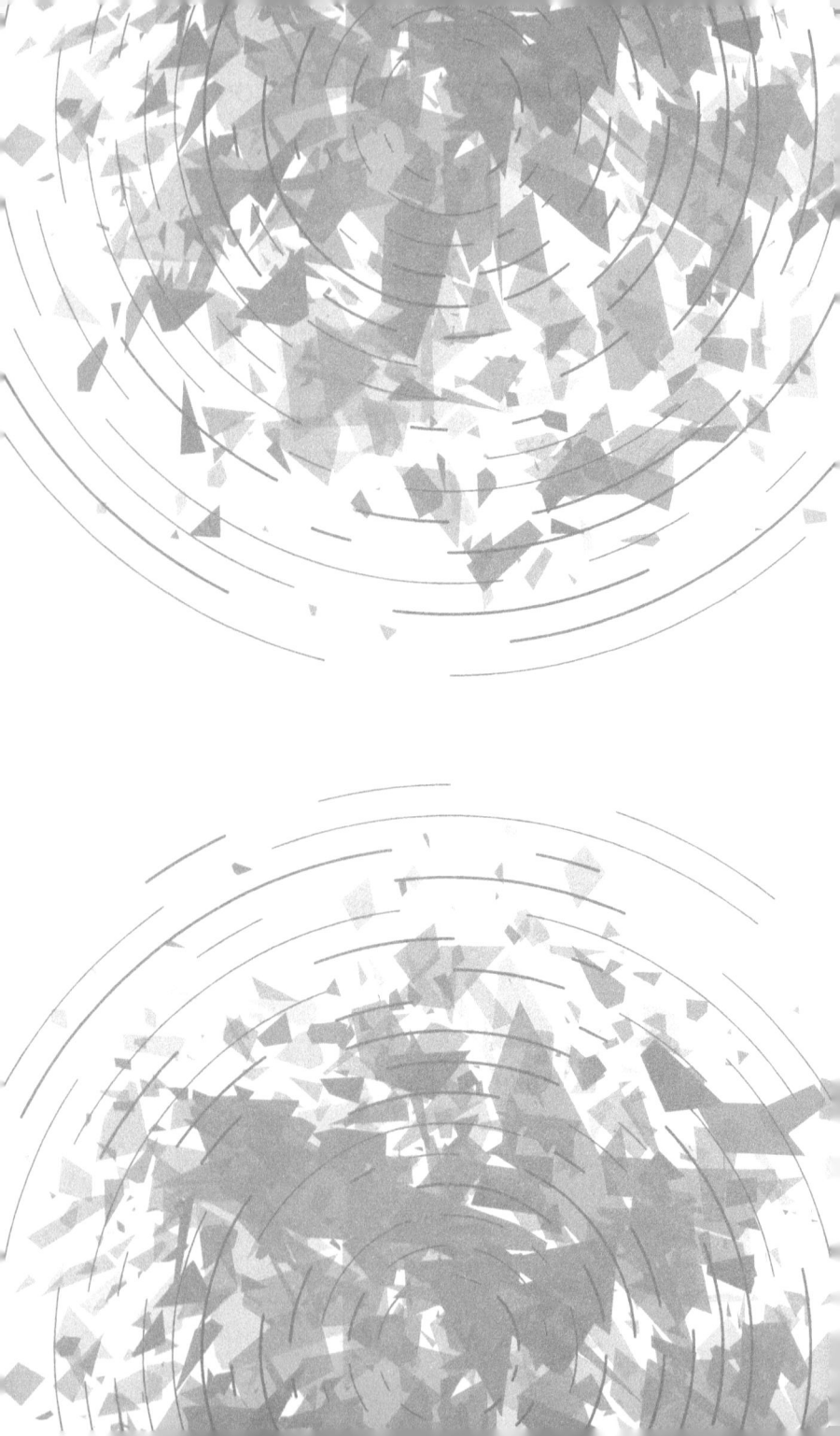

About The Author

CK Westbrook is an environmentalist who lives and works in Washington D.C. and is a self-described old school news junkie. Since the state of our planet and the news are bleak and depressing, Westbrook escapes reality by creating intriguing characters in a science fiction world. The world these characters live in may also be dark and scary, but they do have fantastic adventures that impact their planet. In addition to creating imaginative stories, Westbrook literally breaks free from daily life with an intense passion for travel and has been to all seven continents. Westbrook loves weaving real world topics and crises into suspenseful sci-fi and fantasy. To learn more about CK Westbrook, please go to www.ckwestbrook.com.

www.ingramcontent.com/pod-product-compliance
Lightning Source LLC
Chambersburg PA
CBHW020130120726
47903CB00007B/2188